# *The Audition*

# The Audition

*What will you Sacrifice to live the good life?*

A NOVEL BY
PAUL HIGGINS

authorHOUSE®

*AuthorHouse*™
*1663 Liberty Drive*
*Bloomington, IN 47403*
*www.authorhouse.com*
*Phone: 1-800-839-8640*

*Published by AuthorHouse    05/17/2012*

*ISBN: 978-1-4634-6801-9 (sc)*
*ISBN: 978-1-4634-6802-6 (e)*

For my family

Erika Beck, Jonathan Higgins, and Justin Higgins

Who I love oh so dearly
'Daddies Babies"

And for
Carmen,
Who I deeply miss.

Dedicated in Loving Memory



This book is dedicated to:

Victoria Higgins my sweet dear mother. Through her prayers and unconditional love I was blessed with inner peace and harmony.
(1921-2005)

Robert Clark Higgins, my father, mentor and friend, who showed me how to be a strong black man.
(1926-2002)

Chesteen Higgins my baby sister who I miss so very much. Some day we will be together again as one big happy family. We will toast our reunion with a green apple martini.
(1965-1994)

# ACKNOWLEDGMENT

First and above all I would like to thank my Lord Jesus Christ for the many blessings He has bestowed upon me, and for showing me that good things do come to those who wait. I am truly grateful for all He has done for me.

I would also like to acknowledge:

My mother for all the support she gave me while we were together.

Robert C. Higgins my father who gave me the guidance I needed as I was growing up.

Robin Francis Chesteen Higgins my sister who is, a wonderful parent to my nieces and nephews, Alsha Francis, Mieasha Francis, Reneeah Kilgore, Steven Kilgore, Jasmine Higgins, and Deshawn Higgins who all bring great joy to my life.

My brothers Robert C. Higgins Jr. (Buddy) and Shawn Emaile Higgins.

My daughter Erika Patrice Higgins, my grandchildren Aisha Beck and Braxton Beck.

My first-born son Jonathan Paul Higgins and second son, Justin Higgins.

My cuz, "Big Head" Ann Hooper, Diamond and Daris. Thank you for your support.

My son from another mother Juquari Baskin I love you always and as though you were my own.

Dr.S.T. Williams Jr. My Pastor thank you for keeping me grounded and focused on my spiritual journey.

We all have dreams to do something great in this life.

But first we must prepare ourselves for the journey.

Pray on it.
Claim it.
"Create a blueprint then make it happen."

-P. H. Arbil

# The Audition

What is the greatest Fear Known to Man?

## Success

# PRELUDE

Jonathan Paul had a dream and with that dream he had a plan. From a young child Jonathan had plans on becoming a movie star. When he told his classmates he was going to be a big star one-day laughter rang out all over the playground. Even his close friend told him he was crazy, and that it would never happen. From the beginning the ridicule created self-doubt then hatred set in; he vowed to prove them all wrong. Jonathan had many demons, and he was will to do whatever it took to make a name for himself. In route to his success he meets a beautiful young black district attorney named Jasmine Cooper. Jonathan would later find out that she was married to a Hit-man. Reality has just knocked on his front door causing Jonathan to rethink his plan. Dreams began to resurrect the secrets he had never shared with anyone. They caused him to question the significance of people in his life. Where would these people fit into his plan? How would Jonathan deal with the tragedy that would soon cross his path?

# 16 Days

It's another beautiful day in Hollywood California and the streets are as jammed packed as they are each day, everyone is off to work somewhere in the world of illusion. The "beautiful people" have just started their day on someone's studio lot or set, the assistant director greets you at your trailer where your wardrobe has been laid out for you. After returning from hair and makeup you return to your trailer, upon your arrival the AD has your favorite breakfast waiting on a table along with the shooting schedule and your sides. The food is piping hot you pick over it as you look over your lines, and then you hear a knock on the door.

"Jonathan, we need you on set!" the first AD says.

In the movie business we refer to this as the "S.O.S.D.D", (same old shit different day) also known as the "hurry up to wait game" Someone calls out "Quit on the set! Background! Rolling! And . . . Action!" This continues all day or until the director gets the shot he or she were looking for.

Oh, by the way my name is Jonathan Paul. I'm a six-foot one hundred ninety five pound brown skin black male with hazel brown eyes. I'm built like a gymnast packing twenty-two inch biceps an up and coming actor with big ideas. I've been working in the movie business for about two years now; I started off working behind the scenes as a background performer. It's a shame to say this but without the background performers there would be no movie. I love what I'm doing and the producers know this, so they work your ass off to get the shot they need . . . and then it's a wrap.

You know what's a trip? Some of the main actors who make the big money will not give you the time of day, some will speak to you but others can be assholes to the point that if you even look their way they can have you booted off the set. They'll accuse you of being in their "eye line" distracting them from focusing on their lines. Well I was smart I found out early how the game was played. As time went on I found out who was in charge of giving out contracts to the talent, I sought them out and made friends with them quickly. One day I was Chilin by the craft service table and this cool looking Jewish cat wearing a grey Armani suit with salt and pepper hair approached me. He looked at me up and down and suddenly walked away. I looked at him as though he was crazy and finished hooking my plate up with some fruit and cookies, (Yeah okay I do admit that I'm a sweet junkie) Anyway the dude walked back to where I was standing then he tapped me on the shoulder.

"My name is Marty Cogan just call me Marty. I'm the unit production manager for this show and you are?" said Marty as he reached out his hand to shake mine. "Jonathan Paul" I replied.

"Ok Jonathan, Look I was wondering if you know any karate?" Marty said. "I got some skills what's up?" I Replied.

"The writer of the show just added another character and we we're looking at you to play the part. Providing you have . . . how you put it "Skills" in martial arts" Marty said.

"Yea . . . I know a little something" I said.

"Do you have an agent?" Marty asked.

"Yes I do, his name is Michael Zantex" I replied. Marty raised his eyebrows.

"Michael Zantex . . . he and I go way back, I'm going to call him later to let him know about the changes in your job description. You can go home today and I'll see you Wednesday morning at 7:00 am. Nancy will have a contract waiting for you, and then we can get the ball rolling" Marty said.

My Mother always said just lay low and let God work things out. Marty and I shook hands again, as he walked off he then stopped turned to his right then faced me and said.

"I'll be putting you on a weekly salary of $4500.00. We have sixteen days left on this show, when this show is wrapped I'm going to need you on another project. But we can talk about that later. I'll make sure that Nancy includes a limo and a full size trailer within your contract is that cool?" Marty said.

"Hell yea! That's cool" I replied.

"With an attitude like that you're going to go far in this business. I like you kid" Marty said.

As I head back to my trailer Nancy was waiting for me by the front door she needed to talk to me.

"Jonathan, you have 16 days of work on this project your co-starring with Quawn Lee. Tomorrow you'll meet with Benny in North Hollywood at his gym. Here is all of the Information" Nancy stated as she handed me a slip of paper.

I took the information she wrote and returned to my trailer. As Nancy walked away, I could hear her talking to a production assistant through her headset.

"I'm heading your way now; I need four background players on set now! Send them to hair and makeup . . . you and I will meet with them at wardrobe in two minutes" Nancy said.

Damn landing a gig at $4500.00 a week is an actor's dream. Suddenly I got a text from Michael stating that he just spoke to Marty. Things were looking up, a photo shoot was being set up for me at 3:00 pm and Michael wanted to meet with me. About a week ago he said that I needed to give him new pictures, he was intending on send them out to all the casting directors in town. If you ask me I think this was perfect timing.

As I entered my small studio apartment, I looked around and saw all of the things I had worked so hard for. I said to myself, Thank you Lord for making all things possible. I know my ship is coming in soon. I turned on Neo's song "Closer" I made my way to the bedroom to make sure I had everything I needed; I was set for my photo shoot for this afternoon. I walked to the bathroom to take a nice hot shower; I thought to myself yeah today was a good day.

# THE NEIGHBOR

There was a knock at my front door and standing in front of it was a young black woman, she was about twenty five years of age and introduced herself as Jasmine Cooper. Jasmine was about five feet two inches tall weighed about a hundred and ten pounds. She had bluish green eyes high cheekbones caramel colored skin and dimples that made her look like a doll. She had a body like a brick house 36-24-38. I got out of the shower and headed through my bedroom wearing nothing but a towel she knocked once again.

"Who is it?" I asked.

"Your neighbor from next door" Jasmine replied.

With my hands dripping with body wash I opened the door.

"Hi I'm sorry to bother you" Jasmine said. "I work nights your music sounds good but could you lower it just a little so I get some sleep? Would you mind?" Jasmine replied.

"My bad I didn't realize it was that loud." I answered.

"I just moved in last week and I'm still trying to get settled in" Jasmine introduced herself.

"Jonathan Paul . . . It's a pleasure" I told her.

"No, the pleasure is mine!" Jasmine replied.

As Jasmine extended her hand out to shake mine, I tried to wipe my hands off on the towel. As I grabbed her hand my towel fell to the ground, now I'm standing nude in my doorway. Jasmine looked down at my "family business" then smiled confidently. As she knelt down to pick up my towel she looked into my eyes as she slowly raised up from the floor handing me my towel. Quickly I covered myself with my hands, just in case someone like Ms. Hattie the door popper from across the way saw more than they should have.

"Nice abs maybe you and I can work out together sometimes" Jasmine said.

Jasmine walked off with a smile on her face from ear to ear. I grabbed my towel and tightened it around my waist. I glanced across the hallway and saw Ms. Hattie she was standing in her doorway just looking at me. Ms. Hattie is an elderly rich white woman in her early eighties, she had a big smile on her face I bet she saw the whole thing.

"How you doing young man? Ah . . . if you find the time can you look at my sink later? It's a little clogged up . . . Do you think you could fix it for me?" Ms. Hattie said.

"You may want to call management and let them know about your sink. They'll send someone out to fix it for you I'm sure" I replied.

"Ok I'll call management right now" Ms. Hattie replied.

I closed my door as I left Mrs. Hattie standing in her doorway. She was really trying to get an eye full of some boy candy; I bet she hadn't seen that part of the male anatomy in a long time.

I walked over to my CD player and turned my music down. I look over at the clock on the wall; it read 11:00 am. Suddenly the phone rang. It was Mike my agent calling to give me direction to my photo shoot. Sometimes life has a way of showing you the good things we tend not take notice of. It could be right under our noses and we seam to always think the grass is greener on the other side. But if we just stand still and listen to our spirit, it will guide us in the right direction. In this short wonderful life that we live in, we tend to take things for granted. We are just here for a moment so we have to live life well; because tomorrow is not promised to anyone.

"Damn, now that's the kind ass I like" Jonathan said into the phone.

"What did you say?" Mike asked.

"Just thinking out loud . . . I'll see you at three" I replied.

# REAL TALK

Ok, I'm good to go I'm finished dressing. So I grabbed my garment bag and headed out of the door. I had to make a stop at the barbershop before arriving to the photo shoot. As I pulled into the parking lot of Lennium12 Barber Shop, I noticed a homeless woman eating out of the trash can. I shut off the engine and just watched her as she dug into the trash can. She grabbed a brown paper bag opened it up then started eating a half-eaten hamburger from it, at that moment I got a real good look at her.

"I know her, "That's Malinda Jackson my twelfth grade sweetheart. Damn what happen to her?" I thought to myself.

I got out of my car and began walking towards her. Malinda stopped and looked at me with this crazed look in her eyes. Her hair was all matted and she looked like she had not bathed in months. Her skin was leathery and wrinkled; her fingernails were long and filled with dirt. Slightly bent over her long red dirty trench coat swayed with every movement she made. As I stepped closer we looked into each other's eyes, I saw hell burning in her soul. I could tell she had been on the streets for years and that the drugs had beaten her down to the point that she had lost her self-worth. Hijacked by the night demon TEMPTATION. The lights were on but no one was home Malinda had no idea who I was. All memory of what we once meant to each other was gone. I reached into my pocket pulled out a money clip, and peeled off a hundred dollars bill then I handed it to her. Malinda looked at me with her head tilted she was ticking and twitching like a curious wild animal. She snatched the money from my hand and walked off talking to herself. She looked back at me as she made her way down the street with a limp. It hurt me to my soul to see Malinda in that condition, but the worst part was the fact that she didn't even recognize me . . . Or did she?

"My GOD MALINDA! What the hell happen to you?" I thought.

I dropped my head, and then started walking towards the barbershop wiping my eyes in disbelief as I entered the shop.

Standing behind a chair was my barber, a tall black man with a contagious smile. Dude had this way about him, he always spoke with concern in his voice; I really like that about him.

"You alright Dog?" the barber said to me.

"Na man I just saw something that blew me away" I replied.

"What did you see black man?" asked the barber.

"I just saw my old high school girlfriend digging in a trash can. She was eating from a brown paper bag. And you know what? She looked right at me, and didn't even know who I was" I told him.

"Hey man, those drugs will kick your ass! I was a victim of crack in the late eighties. I lost my wife and kids behind that stuff. Just as soon as I got off that shit my baby sister started messing with it. Her name was Justine Adams; she worked the graveyard shift for Snap Foods. Well, my Mother use to kept my sister kids until she got off work. One day when my sister didn't show up to get her kids; my younger sister who is five years younger than me went to her apartment to see what happened. The two of them had lived together at one time. When Robin moved out, she kept the key to Justine apartment. When Robin opened the door to the apartment she entered the bedroom and found Justine lying across her bed with a crack pipe next to her. A baggie half full of rock cocaine was sitting on her nightstand. The coroner said the crack was too much for her heart to take" the barber told me.

"Sorry to hear that about your sister man, Damn that's messed up!" I replied.

The barber continued with his story. "I asked God to help me find myself and to help me get me closer to Him, it was hard at first but I got through it with his help. Now I'm back in church and I have my shop, I talk to my boys every day they live in New York with their mother. I've been clean now for seventeen years" Said the barber.

"Is that right man? That's great man you just don't know what people are going through these days" I told him.

"You really don't man, that's why I tell people no matter where I am to have a great day. Then I give them a little smile, it kind of keeps them pushin you know. Sometimes I might even give them a hug, because there are days when I'm the one who really needs one. If I don't get a hug from somebody, my whole day could be all fucked up!" The barber told me.

"Dig that, I feel you dog that's real talk" I replied.

The barber continued, "Crack is like a bullet, it has no name on it and it don't care who it takes down, when it hits you, it knocks you on your ass. And boy let me tell you; it's hard to get up from a hit like that no pun intended. "So, how's that acting thing working out for you Dog?" The barber asked.

"It's good to me man I'm lovin it" I replied.

"Hey man, one of my customers is giving a party in the Hollywood Hills this weekend, she's a casting director. You might want to hook up with this female she's doing big things. Her name is Connie Speed, I'll talk to my boy and see if he can hook you up" the barber said.

"I know her! She hooked up my boy Ron Slimmer with "All My Baby's Mamas" That was a good movie, shit . . . that dude was serious about having some kids" I told him.

The barber replied, "The cold thing about dude was, that the women who would have his kids had to be fine. Man! After I saw that movie, I stepped up my game big time. I'm not goanna bring any ugly kids in this world" The barber said.

The barber took the cape from around my neck and started brushing off the stray hair on my face and neck. Behind him there on his workstation he picked up a bottle of his newly stocked cologne, from Shawn Bones "Freak Daddy" collection. He splashed a bit it into the palms of his hand, and then rubbed some on my neck and side burns.

"Damn man! What's the name of that shit? It smells good" I told the barber.

"It's called Freak Daddy it's one of the newest from the Shawn Bones collection. I picked it up this morning and guess what? It's not even out on the market yet, but let me hook you up it's on the house dog" he said as he handed me a small bottle.

I reached into my pocket to pay the barber. And you know what he ignored me. I couldn't believe it, and then he told me to get out of the chair.

"I said it was on the house man. Now get your ass up out of my chair so I cut these little brothas up! Don't you have some place you need to be? Look, your money's no good in here, so I'll see you this weekend. Jonathan, you have a good day my brotha" the barber said to me.

I walked over to the barber's workstation, and laid some money down anyway. I picked up his mirror, looked at the cut, then gave him some dap as I exited out of the back door of the barbershop. I then headed towards the parking lot with a smile on my face got in my car and drove off.

We really don't know very much about people we see every day. They walk around acting like they got it all under control; you never know what people are going through in life or what roads they have been down. Some people follow their dreams, and others have none to follow. There are those who see you trying to come up, and they lay in the cut hating on you hoping and praying that you'll fall flat on your face. We all have gifts that God has given us, if we don't use them he'll just take it away. Then give your gifts to someone else who will use them to make the world a better place. Now, that's real talk.

# THE PHOTO SHOOT

I pulled up into the parking lot of the photo studio. Parked then entered the building. After signing in at the front desk, I followed a bright yellow arrow along the wall to the rear of the building to Stage Four. Upon entering the room through an old rusty doorway, the assistant director approached me.

"You're Jonathan Paul?" the assistant director asked.

"Yes I am and you are . . . ?" I replied.

"Tina the 1st AD ok, come with me and I'll take you to your dressing room. Josh is not ready for you quite yet, so put your first set of cloths on and I'll come back to take you to make up. You don't need to have anything done to your hair; it looks great so just hang out at the craft service table over to my right. When we're ready I'll come and get you" Tina instructed.

At that very moment Mike walked in the studio. He was talking loud to someone on his cell phone. Mike talks to everyone in this manner, but I have to keep him in check, He doesn't pull that shit with me I'll get ass told. His name is Mike Zantex; he kind of put you in the mind of Danny DeVito only taller.

"I'm with him now . . . Well, they are just going to have to wait until the pictures are ready. Let me deal with what? I don't care" Mike said into his cell phone.

People at the craft service table, exchanged looks to one another as Mike raved on in a high-pitched voice. Mike is the type of person who wants things done right away, and doesn't care who he hurts in the process. However he does get things done and makes things happen.

"Don't worry about that! Don't worry about that Tammy . . . what time did Marty say he wanted Jonathan there? Ok I'll have him there 6:00 am on Wednesday? Supreme lot . . . Stage 30? His call time has been moved up to 7:00 pm . . . it's a night shoot. Don't worry about nothing

we'll get the pictures to them by next week . . . talk to you later BYE!"
Mike said to Tammy.

While he was chewing Tammy out, I updated my phone with my new
call time for the Quawn Project.

"Those guys at Supreme think they're slick. They owe me some favors.
I hooked them up with some good talent last year, so now it's time for me
to see some kickbacks!" Mike stated.

I had no idea what Mike was ranting and raving about. But whatever
it was it sounded good to me. I did wonder what he meant, when he said
something about "Those guys at Supreme studios thinking they're slick".
What was that all about? Mike walked over to me. Put his arm on my
shoulder, and then pulled me in close to his chest, in effort to reassure me
that I had nothing to worry about.

"Let me shed some light on the situation. This is what the movie
business is all about. Hypothetically speaking, I do something for you,
and you do something for me. You understand?" Mike said to me.

Mike then pulled up a chair, placed his foot on top of it, then began to
give me his idea of the rundown about the movie business. I kind of had
an idea of what Mike was talking about, I'd heard about the horror stories
that didn't have happy endings for many.

"Listen to me kid, I will not steer you wrong Have I yet? Hear me
when I tell you this . . . You see, everything stems around favors. Look at
it this way, seventy percent is all about favors, and the other thirty percent
is based on talent. That seventy percent is based upon whether they like
you or not, if they like you then you're in" Mike explained to me.

I had this perplexed look on my face. And I didn't' really catch what
mike was trying to say. I felt as though that Mike was trying to provide
me with small bites of a very big picture that could be very hard to digest.
But it was a good thing. "Here is another way to imagine the scope of
things . . . Once again HYPOTHETICALLY speaking. Money marries
money; Boy gets girl and whatever else that falls in the middle. Give
them what they want, and the world is yours. Now under the present
circumstances that was FYI, so don't ever let anyone know what I just told
you, because I will deny every bit of it. Just remember what I said, and it
will all come together for you in time. If you believe little of what you see,
and less of what you hear you'll be just fine" Mike added.

Just then the assistant director arrived, "Jonathan we'll be ready for you in five minutes, I'll come back to get you and we'll go to make up then on to the set".

"Sounds good to me" I responded.

"Your goanna go far in this business kid. You and I are goanna make lots of money together. I have two checks here for you; one is from Lombard studios, and the other is from Brookstone Entertainment. You have three more on their way; you're goanna get there soon enough. Just stay on point and work hard and stay focused" Mike advised.

I felt as though I had been pretty busy for the past two years. I was starting to make a name for myself in Hollywood. I had been doing well by working three days a week, it was time for me to step up my game. I knew that I was only scratching the surface, and there was much more meat on the bone to deal with.

It was a short drive back to my place. But I had some time to get my game plan together. I had to center my thoughts before I could get what I wanted, I thought about what Mike was talking about at the photo shoot, and I knew how I was going to play this game. When I was coming up as a child I would always hear my Mother say When in Rome do as the Romans do.

Now I hear her words loud and clear. I have to be just like them to beat them at their own game. But what will I have to sacrifice to get what I want? That's the question that remained in my mind as I prepared my blueprint for success. As they say in the Bizz; it's about whatever works for you . . .

# SPANK ME

It's nice to get out and drive around the city. Do some serious people watching, people do some strange things just to get the attention that they are lacking in their lives. It's all about what works for you to make your life complete. We have choices, some can help you come up, and others will send you crashing right back down to earth. What's so funny about life is that shit happens. Sometimes we can control the things that we experience, and other times we are not as fortunate.

From a young age I was taught to be nice to people. And to treat them in the same manner in which I wanted to be treated. I was taught not to say hurtful things that I would later regret. In this game that I was about to play, fairness did not exist. Expressions of crudeness and ruthlessness all set in; as you buck you're eyes, only to show your white bright thirty twos. But that's part of the game dog, but you don't hear me though.

Everyone tries to make a fast buck in the entertainment world. The goal is to be seen or heard and to be first at the top by any means necessary. Life is a bitch, and after a person dies they just become a faint memory.

As I came to a complete stop at La Brea and Melrose, I looked across the street and saw a long line of people in front of Pinks Hot Dog Stand. They were all waiting to place their order. I decided to join them. As I pulled into the driveway the parking attendant directed me to park near the outdoor patio. The air was filled with the scent of hot dogs, hamburgers perfume, wealth and opportunity. I made my way over to the line to place my order, and discovered Jasmine my neighbor standing nearby. She seemed to be directing all of her attention on her I-Phone. She was texting away hardly noticing my arrival.

"Hello Jasmine! May I join you?" I asked.

Jasmine looked up with those soft pretty bluish green eyes. I had become lost looking into the windows of her soul. The sensual magnetic lustful look in her eyes caused us to immediately connect. When Jasmine put her iPhone away in my head I heard her soft sexy voice say "I want you"

"You're so sweet I'll have whatever you ordering" she said.

"I'm ordering two chili cheese dog's some curly fries and two root beers" I said.

"How did you know I like chili cheese dogs?" she asked.

"A little birdie flew down and whispered in my ear and told me what you like" I said.

"Is that right? What else did that little birdie tell you?" Jasmine said as she looked up at me from the corner of her eye.

I took her by her warm soft hand and gently pulled her towards me. While looking into her eyes, I slowly ran my fingers through her silky hair. I leaned in, and then planted a soft tender kiss on her wet quivering red lips. An older couple was standing behind us. They looked on, as they reminisced about the time when they expressed themselves to one another in the same way. Through our lips, we communicated the passion we felt for each other. The elderly man tapped me lightly on the shoulder. "Young man the line is moving" he said.

Jasmine and I slowly disengaged then walked over to the window and placed our order. At this point she announced that our dinner was her treat. Almost immediately the cook placed our order on a tray. Jasmine took the tray from the counter and we walked towards the patio in back of the restaurant.

"Tell me about Jasmine" I said.

"What would you like to know about Jasmine?" she replied.

"Well, does she have someone special in your life? What kind of work does she do? And why did she kiss me?" I asked.

"Well, she's single and works for the District Attorney's office as a public defender, but if she remembers correctly you kissed her" she said.

As Jasmine unwrapped one of the chili dog she slid her chair closer to mine. She held the chili cheese dog up, and then placed it close to my mouth. I looked into her eyes and opened my mouth. As I took a bite, with a napkin she wiped the mustard from the Conner of my mouth.

"What else would you like to know about Jasmine?" she said.

"Well, now that you've asked I'm wondering why she doesn't have a man. She's beautiful independent and you seem to know what she wants" I replied.

"Actually, she was engaged to a fella back in Texas. They were together for about two years until he decided he needed to find himself. He broke off the engagement, and then Jasmine moved to LA about six months ago. After living with her aunt in Baldwin Hills for a while she learned that two woman with strong personalities can't live together so she decided to move out. Soon after that she found herself living next door to Jonathan" Jasmine said.

Jasmine took a straw placed it in my cup and took a few sips. As she fixed her eyes upon my lips, she placed the straw in my mouth, and watched me as I sipped on the root beer through the straw.

"I know a good man when I see one. My mama didn't raise any fools. You're right I do know what I want . . . I want you to kiss me again" she said softly.

I kissed her sweet red lips as she closed her eyes. Jasmine all but melted in my arms.

"Boy . . . you're dangerous!" she said as she pulled away.

"You haven't seen NOTHING YET" I replied.

As I got up from the table I got behind Jasmine's chair to help her up. I couldn't help but noticed her well-kept pedicure feet and her full voluptuous breast. As she stood up, her sundress clung gracefully to her well-proportioned body. Damn, her shit looked real good from where I was standing. As we walked towards the car I couldn't keep my eyes off of her ass. I opened the door, and marveled at her backside and then handed the parking attendant a tip as I drove off.

It was August 14, 2009 Jasmine and I were cruising down Melrose Boulevard in my 2010 steel grey Jag. The air was filled with the sweet scent of honeysuckle. The moon shined brightly through the warm summer's night. I stopped at the corner liquor store and picked up a bottle of Merlot, then made our way through the underground parking lot of my gated townhouse. We entered the elevator, got off on the third floor, and headed for my apartment.

As I put my key in the door, Mrs. Hattie the door popper cracked open her door again then watched Jasmine and I as we entered my apartment. Jasmine loved the layout of my apartment. She took a seat on the couch facing the fireplace. Jasmine noticed a picture of a beautiful black woman sitting on the mantel, along with awards from various film projects. I entered the room with our wine glasses and a bottle of Merlot under my arm. I sat the wine glasses down on the glass coffee table, grabbed a couple of pillows threw them on the floor by her feet, and then sat down next to her.

"Come down here and sit next to me" I said softly.

Jasmine slid down onto the floor next to me. I grabbed the remote control and turned on the gas fireplace, then the CD player with Maxwell singing "Pretty Wings" in the background.

"I see we have a lot in common! I love Maxwell is that his new release?" Jasmine asked.

"Yea, I picked it up a few days ago" I replied.

I proceeded to light the candles that were placed about the room. Then I took my place on the pillow next to her. I opened the bottle of Merlot, poured a glass for her, and one for myself.

"I love this song. It reminds me of my Dad when he'd sing me a lullaby"

I handed Jasmine her glass and I picked up mine to make a toast.

"To us my pretty angel Friends forever" I said softly.

Jasmine took a sip from her glass, looked at me then placed her glass on the coffee table. She stood up then unbuttoned her summer dress. As it gently fell to the ground, I stood up and allowed Jasmine to unbuckle my pants. She then proceeded to unbutton my shirt. I placed my wine glass on the coffee table; we embraced one another then engaged in a passionate kiss.

As I kissed her gently on the neck, then her shoulders, Jasmine's head rolled back allowing me to tenderly kiss her breast. Gently I turned her body around, and then kissed her sweet caramel-brown skin on her back. To my delight I discovered a beautiful tattoo on the center of her lower back it read, "Spank Me." As I kissed her 38 specials I gave her a quick spanks on her backside.

"Oooo Yes . . . Spank me Daddy!" Jasmine begged.

Jasmine lowered herself to the ground to face me. I slid myself on top of her and kissed her passionately on the lips. I made my way slowly down to her navel, planting soft kisses along the way. As she raised her legs, my lips met her calves as she welcomed my kisses to the inside of her thighs. I began to gently work my way up to her navel. Jasmine took two short deep breaths, and then released the warmth of her sigh on my skin as we looked into each other's eyes. I moved in closer to her face, planting kisses on her forehead and nose. After kissing the side of her neck, we laid motionless on the floor in a spoon position. The soothing flames from the fireplace, danced on our birthday suites as I whispered in her ear, "Did you like that baby?"

"Yes . . . yes" she cooed.

"Did your old boy ever hook you up like?" I asked.

"He didn't get down like that it was against his religion" she replied.

"Against his Religion? When you love someone, you make love to every part of the body. You unselfishly give them total pleasure, and make love to the mind as well" I replied.

"Is that right? What do you want from me?" Jasmine inquired.

"I want to get to know Jasmine. You're sweet and we like the same things plus I enjoy being with you" I replied.

"You would never hurt me would you?" she questioned.

"Hurt you? I would never lay a hand on you! If I were ever angry with you, I would leave and then later we would talk about it. I would work on us understanding each other little better . . . why did you ask me that?" I replied.

"I didn't tell you the truth about me and dude . . . I was in an abusive relationship with my fiancé. And If I wouldn't say the right things around his friends, he'd say and do all kinds of mean things to me. He would call me dumb, stupid and say the only thing I was good for was a good lay" Jasmine said.

Jasmine continued, "He'd beat my Ass up if he thought I was playing around on him. Sometimes I would have to work late, and he'd start in on me as soon as I got home. Then beatings came, when he was done he'd force me to have sex with him. One night I was sleeping in the nude, he came home drunk with his friends. He pulled the covers off of me and told them, "Look at that shit! That's what I sleep with every night" said Jasmine.

"It's a good thing you got out when you did. Now you have me to protect you and keep you safe" I said reassuringly.

"I DO feel safe with you Jonathan. Hold me tight and tell me that again" Jasmine said in a worried voice.

"I'll protect you Jasmine; you will always be safe with me" I proclaimed.

"Oooo . . . Spank me again daddy" As she softly whispered into my ear.

# BENNY'S GYM

It was a warm morning on August 15th 2009. I was on my way to Benny's Gym for a workout with Quawn Lee. The studio wanted Benny to prepare us for the fight scenes in my upcoming film. Benny was a four-time world champ in full contact karate. When he retired, later he would join the Stunt-Man's Union only to star in a few movies himself. Benny would say that his best work was behind the scenes. We had crossed each other's paths one day on the set of "Con's—in the Air", where he worked out of a trailer at West Hollywood studios.

Benny worked on complicated fight scenes with the main characters. If we needed to look pumped up and buffed, we would lift weights for an hour before the camera rolled. The prop guy prepped us by putting a little dirt on our cloths. Then he would spray us down with water, and then ripped our shirts up to make us look like we were in a knock down drag out fight. When it was quit on the set you'd hear, "Background . . . . sound . . . . rolling . . . . and . . . . action!"

I entered the gym and found Benny in the ring with one of his sparring partners. The gym was filled with punching bags, and full contact fighting gear that hung on the walls. It was complete with everything; a fighter would need in preparation for a fight.

Benny danced around the ring blocking punches that the fighter was throwing at him. With his right leg the sparring partner shot a front snap kick to Benny's chest. Benny slapped it with his right hand. He stepped back, made contact with his opponent's leg then with lightning speed Benny did a reverse spin kick. It caught his partner on the left side of his face, knocking him to the canvas.

"Damn Benny! What you trying to do kill the man?" I said.

"Hey Jonathan! You're early! Aw he's a tough guy he can handle it. Did you bring your script with you?" Benny asked.

"Yea, I brought it with me . . . You know what? If you'd kick me like that I'd have to cut YOU Dog . . ." I replied.

Benny climbed out of the ring jumped to the floor and walked over to me and gave me a hug.

"So you're moving up in the business Hun? That's a good thing. Marty called me yesterday evening and said you have two big scenes with Lee. He wants you to look good for of the camera. I told him not to worry about a thing; I'm going to hook you up. Lee couldn't make it, so it just you and I today" Benny said.

Benny motioned for me to follow him, as we entered his office. Not long before I arrived, a messenger had just delivered the script.

"Ok, let's see what we have here" Benny said as he settled into his large comfortable chair.

We opened our scripts to the first fight scene. Benny proceeded to explain, that he needed me to look as good, or even better than Bruce Lee. By doing that, it could lead to more film projects.

"This is what I'd like to do", Benny continued, "Let's read all the action parts. That way I can see what needs to be improved. First of all, we need to go through every movement as slowly as possible. When the producers and I decide that it looks good, we'll be ready for picture" Benny said.

As we left his office headed for the gym, Benny began to break down the details of each scene with me. The gym was filled with some of the usual guys that he uses in some of his film projects. After the introductions, Benny explained that he wanted us to work together to create, various complexed fight scenes.

"Ok, let's start playing around with this and see where it leads. I want these scenes to be powerful! You understand? You and Lee can work out the rest between the two of you. After that, I'll make some adjustments for the camera. I want the fight scene to look believable . . . You know what I mean?" he said.

This opportunity was a dream come true for me. I hung on to my dreams, even though hurtful things were said to me by many people who had no focus on their own realities, I stayed strong. There have been many shows where I've watched other actors as they worked with the stunt coordinator. It was exciting for me to finally have a shot at it myself. Doing my own stunts as a leading man in a feature film amazed me beyond belief. I couldn't think of anything better than having the opportunity to make money while having fun. My childhood classmates would love to hear about this! Not . . . I could still hear their taunting, "You aren't going to be nothing! You can't even read. You walking around here telling people you're going to be this big star, Boy you don't know what you're talking about. You crazy! Ha . . . you couldn't act yourself out of a wet paper bag."

Reading was difficult for me when I was in grade school. I was terrified, when the teacher would make me read out loud in front of the classroom. I needed glasses, and I couldn't focus on what I was reading. The words just wouldn't stop moving on the pages. I had to tolerate ridicule, and taunting from my classmates on a daily basis. From an early age that's when I decided that I was going to prove them all wrong. I spent much of my life trying to accomplish this. It wasn't until later in life when I discovered, that the only person I really needed to prove anything to, was the man in the mirror ME.

I could tell that Benny liked who I was as a person. He had faith in me, and knew that I was ready for this role. I was hungry and confident, and focused on meeting this challenge face to face.

For a moment I reflected on the past. And all the things that brought me to this point in my life. I needed to get my feet wet no matter how painful things may get. We must plan our destiny I was driven to accomplish something in this industry that no one else had ever done before. My dream was to be more successful, than Yul Brenner, Charlton Heston, Samuel Jackson, Sydney Portier and Denzel Washington.

"Jonathan, JONATHAN! Are you alright?" Benny said. "I'm fine I just had a long night, got a lot on my mind I'm good. What were you saying about making adjustments for the camera?" I asked as I brought myself back into the moment.

"When we work out all the angles I want to set you up with a cable and harness. This will add to the effect, we want and make you look like you're doing some Matrix shit you know what I mean?" Benny said. "I feel you" Jonathan said.

"After we finish shooting the entire scene, we'll run it through (CGI) a computer generated integration program" Benny said excitedly.

Benny patted me on the shoulder as we shook hands. We both felt, this would be a piece of cake. There were adjustments to be made in the shooting schedule, as indicated by a note attached to the script.

"Look, I got a message from Marty today. He said the producers moved the shooting schedule up. They want to shoot your scenes with Lee two weeks from today. But that's a good thing because now everything will be fresh in your mind . . . Cool" Benny said.

"Yeah, that's cool this will give me a chance to have all eyes on me, and then show them what I'm really workin with" I replied. "Were good for today?" He asked.

"Yeah, we're good, I'll see you tomorrow same time." I replied. What's the rush? You have a hot date?" Benny asked.

"Nah, it's not like that, I have an audition at 2:00 Dog" I replied.

"Ok then, do your thing man get that money. I'll see you here tomorrow at ten am" Benny said.

One day I thought I had a role locked down contracts were signed and shooting dates was set. Then I get a phone call that the show was canceled. There are so many disappointments in this business. Stuck on stupid that's not an option. In this game you got to keep it pushin, because when one door closes another one opens. But now if you wait too long they'll forget all about you.

# AUNT MINNIE

Here we go again; I should have already learned after two years of being in the business I should be over this crap. It's always the same old shit, right before I walk in to a casting director's office I get the bubble guts. I need to learn to calm down and gather my thoughts. But something seemed a little different today from other auditions. I had two hours to kill so I decided to have a cup of coffee and a cigarette that should help me chill out.

Suddenly the phone rang I glanced down at my caller ID it was my Aunt Minnie calling from Texas. Aunt Minnie checks on me at least three times a week. She's been my rock since the passing of my mother in 2005. Aunt Minnie has been there for me, especially during the times when I've had difficulty in keeping it all together. "Hello Auntie! How you doing?" I said as I picked up the phone.

"I'm doing fine baby what's wrong? I can hear it in your voice" she replied.

"Oh, I don't know Auntie sometimes it's tough for me, I just don't know what's wrong" I answered.

"Boy! You know I know you better than that you can't fool me." Aunt Mamie responded.

"I have an audition today Auntie and . . . I don't think" I started to explain.

"Shut your mouth boy! You're going to do just fine. Now think about all the hard work you've done to get where you are today. I'm so proud of you Jonathan. Just the other night Brenda's boy was telling me that he had a class where they were looking at a DVD to get some extra credit and guess what? It was a movie you stared in "The Body Count" Brenda's boy was so proud to tell his classmates that the star of that movie was his uncle. You should have seen him, his face lit up when he was telling me what had happened. We love you JP and we'll support you no matter what you do" she assured me.

As my face fell I looked toward the fireplace where my Mothers picture sat. As I listened to Auntie I focused on my mother's picture and tears began to roll down my face. "Are you listening to me?" Aunt Minnie said.

"Yes Ma'am, I hear you" I responded with my voice cracking. Aunt Minnie could tell I was crying.

"Listen baby, you pick yourself up, and dust yourself off then get your head right. It's going to be alright, I know you're going to do just fine" she said.

"But . . . but" I began.

"Jonathan Paul! Nothing will ever stand in your way. GOD has a plan for you. This is your time to shine son if only your Mother were still alive she would tell you "STAND UP AND BE A MAN" take it to GOD, and then get out of your own way. Let him work it out for you, do you hear what I'm saying baby? You can't do it all by yourself Give it to GOD, and let it go" she pleaded.

I tried to hold myself together but the tears wouldn't stop running down my face. The more I tried to stop the tears the more they fell. I knew what Auntie was telling me was truth.

"Let it go baby," she continued. If you want to cry go ahead I understand. It's not just about the audition you miss your mother and you want her to see your success I miss her too. But know one thing she will always be with you, she's smiling at you as we speak" Aunt Minnie said softly into the phone.

"Aunt Minnie, this is one of the biggest auditions of my life. I have to read for one of the biggest casting director in Hollywood. I want this to work out for me so bad it hurts. I use to talk to mom before an audition, and just to hear her voice made everything ok. Mom would make me feel as though I was on top of the world. She used to tell me THE WORLD WAS MINE I believed her because she believed IN ME" I told Aunt Minnie.

"The world IS yours and she is STILL with you. If you listen real closely you can hear her speak to you. Just follow your heart baby OK. Now let's just say you DON'T get the part it's not the end of the world. This just means that GOD just has something else better in mind for you, so you remember that!" Aunt Minnie continued.

At that moment Aunt Minnie sounded just like my mother she was making a lot of sense. I knew what she was telling me was right, but it hurt me deep down in my soul to hear it. I needed those words of assurance, because what I was about to face could be too much for me to bear.

"I want to thank you for being there for me Auntie" I told her. "I needed to hear that. What doesn't kill you will make you stronger right? I love you from the bottom of my heart Auntie" I said.

"I love you too baby. Now you keep your head up, and always stay prayed up, if you do this you will never go wrong." Aunt Minnie took a deep breath and said "Well, I need to fix me something to eat then take my blood pressure pills, and wash some cloths for Breads boy. With his mom trying to hold down two jobs and going to school it gets rough on her at times. So I do what can to help her out around the house. JP, you're gonna be just fine. Call me later and let me know how your audition went ok baby, I Love you." Aunt Minnie said.

"Okay auntie . . . I love you more" I told her as I hung up the phone.

The talk with Aunt Minnie was just what I needed. It allowed me to reflect on a lot of things in my life. It became very clear in my mind, what Mike was telling me. I had to beat them at their own game. When it's all said and done I can look back at my life and have no regrets. It's been said many times before, the same people you see on your way up that ladder to fame, are the very ones you see coming down, only to crash and burn.

# Godiva Chocolates

It's a mid-day afternoon and I'm ready game on. My first stop will be at the florist to pick out a beautiful bouquet of white roses. I'll also stop at the chocolatier to get some Godiva chocolates for the receptionist she'll really appreciate this. I got this on lock down thanks to the advice of an old man I met on a set one day. I learned that the person you have to impress the most is the receptionist. If you're smooth and get in good with her you are guaranteed to get a pass to see the casting director. She's the first and most important person you need to know in this business, so you must make a good first impression.

The talk with Aunt Minnie gave me the extra boost of confidence that I needed. I pulled up to the main gate at Supreme Studios where a guard was allowing cars to enter on to the lot. As I pulled up along the guards shack his appearance made me laugh. This guy looked like he just stepped out of a Terminator movie. With his clean-cut look, sunglasses black police uniform shiny guard badge, and boots the missing gun was replaced by a nightstick.

"How you doing Bra Man?" I said.

"I'm good sir . . . Where are you going?" the guard inquired.

"The Ruth Ball Building" I replied.

OK sir, Park over there by the bookstore and follow the arrow pointing to the Ruth Ball Building, you can't miss it. Before I left the station I said to the guard, "Can you help me out here? I have a bouquet of roses and some Godiva Chocolates for the receptionist. She told me her name but I forgot it Dog"

"Her name is Sandy, and dude she is Hella fine. Long sandy blond hair, light skin, green eyes, and I mean sista got back for days!" the guard said.

"That's her all day long thanks, you have a good day" I told the guard before driving away.

On this day I was reading for Connie Speed one of the biggest casting directors in Los Angeles. Connie's about 5'4 brown complexion, nice breast, and a banging body. She likes to wear African wraps on her head, and dresses to show off her beautiful shape. I was told that if Connie likes you, you'll never have to look for work again.

I parked my car and followed the signs to the Ruth Ball Building. Before I walked into the office I took some time to gather my composure. It was a typical day at Supreme studios. People were walking around to and from different sets. Some stages had flashing red lights just over the door which meant they were taping. Messengers rode mopeds from studio to studio dropping off dailies (Already shot film footage) to production offices. Everyone was busily rushing around getting their grind on.

When I arrived at Connie's office I opened the door, and the room was filled with guys all waiting to read for Connie. I entered the room closed the door and all eyes were on me. I was sure that everyone was thinking the same thing about one another, hoping that the next guy wouldn't get the part. To me it didn't really matter what anyone thought because in this business it's all about timing and who can run the best game.

I walked over to the receptionist's desk and just as the guard said Sandy was as pretty as she could be. As I approached her desk she looked up at me, and said in a sweet sexy voice, "You're here to read for Connie?" "Yes I am" I replied.

She looks at the bouquet of roses, and the box of Godiva Chocolates. She knew I had spent a lot of money for them, and those chocolates were to die for.

"Those flowers are beautiful! You're going to make someone VERY happy with that!" Sandy said.

"I knew there would be someone like you in here that could appreciate good taste when they saw it" I told Sandy.

"Oh! That so sweet!" she replied.

With a devilish grin on her face Sandy beckoned me to lean towards her. She reached for my right ear lobe, and then whispered "Better ones have tried lines like yours. But check this out home boy you can plant your ass in one of those chairs with everyone else ok. Thank you for the roses, and the box of chocolates" Sandy said softly.

As I laid my picture and resume down on Sandy's desk I handed her the roses and chocolates. I walked away to take a seat next to one of the actors. As I crossed my legs I noticed one guy laughing. I gave him a dirty look Sandy then got up from her desk with pictures in her hand she looked over at me smiled then shook her head as she walked towards casting room.

Sandy entered Connie's office then gently closed the door behind her. At that point I could have cared less about what anyone thought. I knew everyone was feeling the same way and I bet they all want to kick my ass right about now. My game face was on and I came to play. I leaned back in my chair with a relaxed look on my face waiting for my name to be called. Just as I reached for my iPhone to shut it off the casting director's door opened.

"Jonathan, Connie wants to see you" Sandy announced.

I stood up gathered my thoughts then headed towards the opened casting director's door. As I walked past the other guys I couldn't help but notice the expression of amazement on their faces.

As I entered the casting room a number of men were seated at a large round table. Connie was seated at the center of the table. Surrounding her was the Director Jeff Haven, Robert Crition the writer, and her husband Peter the Executive Producer. I noticed them leaning towards each other talking amongst them selves in a very low whisper. When I stepped into the room an uneasy feeling came over me. There was not one pleasant expression on anyone's face something was up I could feel it. At the end of the table was one empty chair I presume for me.

"Jonathan Paul . . . hum, nice name have a seat . . . Great look what you think Jeff?" said Connie.

"Yeah, I like him he's a good-looking kid. I think he is right for the role. Jeff turned to me and said; "I remember working with you on the Craven Project remember that? You were Rashawn's stand-in. I gave you some sides one hour before we started to shoot and you memorized all of his lines I was really impressed. When I saw your picture, I told Connie I thought you'd be the person for this role" Jeff replied.

"Is Mike Zantex your agent?" Peter asked.

"Yes sir he is" I replied.

Connie, Jeff, Robert and Peter all looked at each other. I asked myself "Am I about to be the newest addition to the Supreme Family? What do they have planned for me? Will I make millions for this studio? Or is this just another dry run?"

"Can I get a little personal with you for a moment Jonathan?" Peter asked.

"Well, that depends on how personal you want to get Sir" I replied.

Everybody kind of chuckled at my remark. Peter opened a box of Cuban cigars, and offered one to each of us. Peter lit his cigar took a puff looked at me then got up from his chair and walked over to where I was sitting. He lit my cigar, and then returned to his chair.

"How much did lumbar Pictures pay you for that role you played in The Alternative Killers?" Peter inquired.

"Forty five hundred a week" I replied.

"Forty five hundred a week? A day player . . . Ok get Mike on the phone" Peter ordered.

Connie called Mike from the studio phone that was sitting in the center of the table she puts him on speakerphone.

"Hey Mike . . . I have Jonathan here with me we'd like to sign him to a four-year picture deal starting with twenty million a picture with perks plus your 10%. You cool with that?" Peter said toward the phone.

"Hell yea! I'm cool with that, check this out I have two kids I need you to look at" Mike added.

"Fax me over their pictures and resumes Connie will take it from there . . . Hey Mike how's your putting game?" Peter asked.

"I haven't been going lately but I need to" Mike answered.

"I'm going to hit the green tomorrow morning about 6:30 at the North Hollywood Golf Course. We'll play a few holes do breakfast tie up some loose ends, and see if we need to make any changes you know the deal . . ." Peter said.

"Alright, see you there" Mike said as Peter motioned towards Connie to hang up the phone.

"Well Jonathan that's it you're in. You'll hear from Connie in a couple of days. She'll let you know when you can pick up your script, and when your contract is ready any questions?" Peter asked. "No sir I'm good, I want to thank you all for giving me my first big break I won't let you down" I promised.

"I know you won't, you're a good kid AND I LIKE YOU . . . Welcome to Supreme studios" Jeff said as he shook my hand.

As I made my way towards the door Connie joined me we walked outside stood in the hallway where we continued our conversation.

"Jonathan, get my number from Sandy then call me tomorrow so we can talk OK? Then we'll go from there" she said as we parted ways she returned to the casting room and closed the door.

"I can't believe what just happened in there." I thought to myself as I made my way over to Sandy's desk. I noticed all the guys were still waiting in the hallway to get their chance to read for Connie. Every one of them gave me a dirty look. So I returned their hard stare with a big smile.

Sandy handed me Connie's business card, and her own personal number. "Call me later we can go somewhere and talk. This is not the place to do it if you know what I mean? Big Brother never sleeps around here they hear everything we talk about," she told me. "I feel you. Ok Sandy, I'll call you around eight o'clock tonight" I told her as I walked away.

"Hey, thanks for the roses, and the chocolates" she said with a smile.

It's a shame that big players in this entertainment world sometimes make you have the wrong impression about this business. Many times you may feel that they are not playing fair. You work your ass off to pay thousands of dollars for acting classes, singing lessons, workshops, and seminars. Now don't misunderstand me, it can be a good thing but you can also get CAUGHT UP if you don't have your head on right. The bottom line is how committed are you. You must do your homework research your craft. So when you enter that ring, you better be ready to rock and roll because if you screw up someone else will take your place.

There may be times when you've done all the right things. You've memorized all your lines for your audition, and you raised some eyebrows. What if you get a call back? What if they already knew who had the part? It's cool because the show must go on as they say. Everyone gets a chance to see the casting director at some point, and time in their career. This is a serious cold game, and if you learn to play it you can make some hard cold cash. Sometimes we let the money make us never focusing on how to make the money

# CHOCOLATE SHAKE

It was dust dark Dinner at Melody's Restaurant was always a treat for me. I'm a sucker for good old fashion 1950's Texas down home cooking. On a clear sunny day I would sit on the patio outside in front of the restaurant watching cars zip up and down sunset strip. That was my favorite spot at the restaurant. I enjoyed sipping down an ice cold chocolate shake topped off with real whipped cream and a big red juicy cherry in the center. From that spot one can really get a good view of Hollywood's finest also known as The Beautiful People. They remind me of robots as they walk up and down the sidewalk as though they were on a runway modeling. They window shop while pointing at people as they walk their ten thousand dollar Sharpe's on the strip. They spend thousands of dollars on real diamond collars just for their dogs, in a strange kind of way I liked it. They would stop look then "Vogue" as they keep it pushin down strip. They learn at a very early age how to get that all mighty dollar at any coast.

I called Sandy to see if we were still on for the evening. I arrived at the restaurant about 7:00pm. The waiter came outside gave me a menu then started to stare. I just ignored him and kept reading the menu. Dude was trying figure out where he had seen me before, but I knew he would remember before the evening was over.

"How you doing sir I'm Derrick and I will be your waiter for this evening" he announced. "I'm good and yourself?" I asked.

"Fine thank you, can I get you anything with that chocolate shake?" Asked the waiter.

"I'm waiting on someone once they get here I'll call you" I told the waiter.

Right at that moment he remembered where he saw me. Derrick was a movie buff he must have waited on everyone from Whoopi to Denzel. He knows how entertainers can be at times! Some are approachable and others are just plain assholes. Derrick had this unsure look on his face I make a comment about it.

"You alright Derrick? Look like you have something on your mind . . . You did say your name was Derrick right?" I asked.

"I don't want you to think that I'm a stocker or anything. But I just realized who you were. You're Jonathan Paul right? I have followed every movie you have done for the last two years. I think you're a great actor dude. When you played that roll in The Black Diamond I memorized every fight scene you did in that movie" he said with excitement.

"That's cool dog I'm glad you liked it" I told him.

Derrick just went on and on I thought he would never shut up. It was cool at first then people started looking at me, and pointing in my direction. I was hoping he would kind of just walk away but it was cool.

"I really dug that character you played in Rampage. You were a straight up thug in that movie. You reminded me of a friend of mines father he was in the Watts Riot, and he didn't take no shit from anyone either. What kind of person is Leonard Holland? Is he cool?" Derrick asked.

"Oh! Leonard he's cool man we boxed a little on the set between scenes, and exchanged some ideas we hang out from time to time" I told him.

Sandy entered the restaurant while I was talking to Derrick. I got a little side tracked during the conversation. Derrick noticed that I was looking into the, restaurant and he saw Sandy Heading towards the front door of the joint "is she the person you're waiting for?" Derrick asked.

"Aw man I'm sorry I'm just running my mouth. I couldn't help but notice you looking in the restaurant I'll go and get her for you" Derrick said.

Derrick left then walked in to the restaurant and got Sandy's attention. She turned her head, and saw me out on the patio. With my hand I motioned for her to come join me. It's funny how some people you don't even know can just walk up to you, and read you. It ain't funny but the shits all true, and that can be frightening at times.

I noticed Sandy was wearing her hair differently from the way it was earlier today. This evening she was wearing it up with chopsticks very sexy. I was really digging her Armani outfit. Derrick walked over to the table with Sandy, and apologized for all the questions he was asking. As Derrick spoke I started looking at Sandy's feet, her thighs her waist, then that angelic look she wears on her face . . . so enticing I think I'm in love.

"Let me get you something to drink, what would you like?" Derrick asked.

"What are you drinking Jonathan?" Sandy said.

"A Chocolate Shake" I replied.

"Umm, Let me have a strawberry milkshake with lots of cherries" Sandy said.

"How do you mix cherries, and strawberries?" I asked.

"Because I can" she said.

"Ok be nice, so how you doing this evening?" I asked.

"I'm doing fine now. You know you started some mess today when you left the office I just wanted you to know that" Sandy said.

"What happened? What did I do?" I replied.

When you left today Connie called me into her office and told me to do something that you never ever do at an Audition. Now if the casting director finds the person they were looking for it should be a done deal. But the Screen Actors Guild says that they still have to hold the Audition until everyone has been seen right?" Sandy said.

"I guess I don't know" Jonathan replied.

"Oh did you know Connie was my mother?" Sandy said.

"No, I didn't know that, what are you driving at?" Jonathan replied.

"This woman told me to tell all those angry men that the Audition was over for the day. And that she apprehended them all for coming down. When I said that I thought I was going to have to fight every person in there. One guy said that he was going to call SAG and let them know he did not get a fair chance to read for the role think she gave a dam? HELL NO what Connie wants Connie gets and honey Hollywood loves them some Connie Speed" said Sandy.

Now I know why Connie was so point blank with me she's a very manipulating woman. I think Sandy may have some ways just like her mom, and I like that I like a challenge. I'm going to work this it's all about business. I'll work her to get what I want, and I'll let her work me to get what she wants. The second page of my blue print is almost done It's all coming together Hollywood will never know what hit them.

"So what happened?" I asked.

"Not a damn thang Man! Didn't you know she runs all of the Hollywood Producers in this town? She has them all eating out of the palms of her hands. She tells them who's going to work in this town and who's not. She's the gatekeeper for the industry. And if you cross her you'll be just a memory, and you'll never work a day in Hollywood on anyone's movie set" Sandy said.

"I'm going to keep that in mind that's good to know, so what do you want to eat girl?" I asked.

"You are cuttin up I'm telling you about these snakes, and you talking about food. You have something up your sleeve. I can see it in your face you're up to something" Sandy said.

"What do you dream about?" I asked.

"Now you really lost me. What in the hell are you talking about?" she asked.

The first page of the blue print is done now I can start working on my second page. I REALLY like this girl yep I think I'm in love. I can really see us being married this can really work. Sandy will be the president of my corporation and Connie will be my biggest and most prized investor slash mother-in-law. I needed to make all the pieces fit starting now.

"I'm talking about you and me, there's a reason for everything that happens to us in life. Look, I'm just going to put it out there. I know we just met and all I think I'm in love with you, and we need to hook up" I said.

"Umm . . . is that what you really think? Would the roses and Chocolates have anything to do with this speech?" Sandy replied.

"In a way it does you saw how I was trying to get at you when I first saw you. I knew you were the one for me and my spirit told me you were going to be my wife" I said.

"IS THAT RIGHT? Umm, and what else did your spirit tell you?" Sandy replied.

Sandy got up and slid her chair next to mine. She then snuggled up against me, and grabbed both of my hands.

"I wanna let you know something about me when I get serious about someone I don't play games. I'm focused on just them, and what I need to do to keep them happy. I don't share my man with anyone, and I love real hard. Now if you think you can deal with those options then we can work on this hookin' up thang" she said.

"It's not an option because you and I are on the same page. I know a good thing when I see it. I'm feeling everything about you I can see you, and I doing big things together. I'm focused us being together for a long time. I love long hard, and deep. I play for keeps now can you deal with that?" I said.

Sandy had her head buried into my chest she looked up at my mouth with a burning desire to kiss my lips. We both moved in for a lustful wet passionate kiss. Something happened to Sandy that had never happened to her before. She had a warm rippling sensation in her stomach. Suddenly sandy peeled herself away from my lips, and snuggled into my chest like a cat.

"Oooo wee! Nobody and I mean nobody has ever kissed me like that before! I'm hooked" Sandy said.

"Enough about me I wanna know more about you. You're the first person they talked about in a long time. I'll tell you something they were really impressed with you. They see people every day, and you would hear Connie say, "Can you call this person, or we didn't like that guy." They've been casting for this part for about eight weeks now, and then you came along. I don't know what you did but Connie really likes you. If you be nice I'll tell you all her little secrets" Sandy said.

"Wouldn't that be nice? You do something for me, and I'll do something for you" I said.

"Well, that depends on what you want me to do for you" Sandy replied.

"First let's get away from here. Let's find a place where we can be alone in a more relaxed comfortable setting. Then I can tell you every thing you wanna know about me" I told her.

"Is that's what you really wanna do? Ok, let's go some place where we can RELAX, and GET TO KNOW each other a little better, I'm right behind you" she told me.

The second page of my blue print was now completed. It was time to work on the foundation. When building a strong sturdy structure the footing must be flawless. Everything must be in the right position at the right time. In order for anything to be a success you must have a solid foundation well worked out plan.

# THE HOOK UP

I love the Hollywood nightlife cruising down Hollywood Boulevard. The smell of Skunkweed lingers in the air from a nearby wild party atop of Mount Olympus reminds me of Xmas. Bumping some Michael Jackson's "Smooth Criminal" as Horn's blow laughter everywhere. No one seems to have a worry in the world it's Friday night, and your workweek is over until Monday morning when it's back to that 9 to 5 grind again.

I saw people standing in long lines waiting to get into what they felt was most popular club in the city. I passed by one of Hollywood's famous costume stores on the Boulevard, and on any giving night you would see Mohammad Ali sitting on a stool near the front of the store. You'd see him playing with the kids laughing, and joking with the owner. Ali would Sign autographs or do a simple magic trick with those deadly weapons he uses to beat his opponents to the punch. Those weapons helped rank him as the Heavyweight Champion of the world.

I pulled over parked in front of the store and blew my horn twice. Bernard Jenkins a longtime friend college buddy and roommate stood in the doorway of the store with a big smile on his face. Bernard kind of puts you in the mind of Marlon Wayans a goofy looking brotha always opinionated, and a very out spoken kind of guy. He yelled out my damn name as loud as he could.

"JONATHAN PAUL! What's up my Ninja? As I live and breathe. What's going on with you Roomie? Dam! Who's the pretty girl sitting next to you?" Bernard said.

Bernard works for the studio as a makeup artist during the day then at the costume store at night. Child support was kicking the living shit out of him real tough. So my boy took a second job so he could take better care of his kids. He loves what he does with the studios. When we were in college he, and I would talk about what we would do after we graduated. Bernard has worked on shows like Star Path, Psychiatric Disorder, and Vampire in the Hood. If you needed a great latex job with blood, and cuts on your face Bernard was the man to get the job done. All the studios used Bernard because the brotha was good.

"Sandy met Bernard Jenkins the baddest makeup artist in Hollywood. We were roommates in college, and I had to put up with his loud snoring, and smelly feet for four years" I said.

"Its nice to meet you Bernard" Sandy replied.

"Like wise when did you get this Jag Dog? Sweet hey let me halla at you big brotha Jonathan. There's this short crack head lookin' Oompah Loompah cop that likes to give tickets to customers that park right here. You might wanna move from here, and park in the back I can't stand him. He already gave me three tickets this week plus he had my shit towed . . . YOU PUNK!" Bernard said.

The cop that Bernard was talking about had just rolled by when he yelled out "You punk". Bernard jumped into the back seat of my Jag. The cop slowed down turned around in the middle of the street, and then rolls back in our direction looking at Bernard real hard. But he kept it pushin on down the street.

"Go down the street here at the corner make right. Make another right in the alley, and park in the parking lot I got the hook up" Bernard said.

Bernard pulled out a joint the size of a cigar from his shirt pocket. He lit it then passed it to me it kind of pissed me off.

"Dude! What are you doing man? Don't you see my girl sitting here?" I said.

"SMOKING this bomb ass Kush, Oh you don't smoke anymore my Ninja?" he asked.

"Well if you won't hit it, I will" Sandy said.

"I knew I liked you when I first saw you. Hey Big Homie stop being a weenie" Bernard said.

"Pass me the damn thing then. I know you're not going back in the store smelling like weed dude" I said.

"Nope as of 10:05 I will not have to return to work until Monday. So I'm going to party this weekend, and do me you know why?" Bernard said.

"Why Bernard?" I asked.

"Because, I can NOW WHAT?" he replied.

Sandy looked very familiar to Bernard but he couldn't place where he saw her.

"What do you do Sandy?" Bernard asked.

"I'm a receptionist over at Supreme Studios I work for Connie Speed" she replied.

"Bite me! Is that right? That's where I seen you in the cafeteria. One day this kid rode his moped inside the joint you were walking out, and he ran into you, and you spilled red soda all over your pearl white cashmere sweater BOY! Did you go off . . . ?" Bernard said.

"It was a Michael Kors sweater I paid twelve hundred dollars for it, and it was ruined after that. I gave it to the good will (He He) now I have that little fart doing errands for me. His dad is a big wig on the lot, if he knew his son was riding that moped inside the cafeteria his little five hundred dollar allowance would be taken away. So I black-mailed his little ass" Sandy said.

"See those little rich kids think they can do whatever the hell they want to do, and get away with it. What they need is their little Ass whipped then they'll have more respect for people, and their shit" Bernard said.

"Bernard, are you going to pass that joint or talk all night? We learn to multi-task in this day, and time. See that's the same shit you use to do when we were in college. That's why your ass used to get socked up all the time Puff, Puff pass Ninja" I said.

Bernard passed the joint to Sandy while blowing out a big cloud of smoke and coughing.

"Is that right? This is my weed, and I can do what ever I want to with it Man!" Bernard said

Then you, and your weed can get the HELL up out of my car MAN" I told him.

"NOW! There you go, hey big brotha Jonathan look it's this cat I know that works on the set with me he's giving a party in Bel—Aire tonight ya'll wanna go?" Bernard asked as he winked at Sandy.

"You down baby? I mean we can do something else if you want?" I asked Sandy.

"It's cool as long as I'm with you it doesn't matter. I'm down with it let's roll" Sandy said.

"Now see that's what I'm talking about. I love a woman who is down with her man. I can't seem to find that girl. I always seem to run into those microwave chicks, you know the 'I want it right now' type of girls" Bernard said.

I started the car then drove out of the parking lot the same way we drove in. When I got to Hollywood Boulevard I made a left turn Sandy was schooling Bernard on how to hook up with the right girl.

"Let me give you some advice on how to hook up with the right chick baby. My grandma would always tell me as a little girl don't no man want a woman who always got her hands out. He has eyes if he wants you to have something he'll give it to you. So when the time is right for you to have a mate you'll know it she will too" Sandy said.

"Damn she's wise too Dog! Do you have a sister a friend or a cousin? I like the way you think. This some real shit she's pippin off man she just hit me over the head with some cold old school game . . ." Bernard said.

Bernard has not changed. The moment he gets weed into his system that brother will never shut up. I love him like he was my own brother. There's nothing in this world I wouldn't do for him that's my dog. As I looked in my rear view mirror I could see clusters of lights closing in to the back of my car. It was some motorcycle riders they were riding in twos, and had to been doing at least seventy as they zoomed by. Sandy passed me the joint as I took a nice long drag this biker dude shot past me so fast I almost swallowed the joint. Dude was mashing he was doing at least 110 easy. He cut to the right almost cutting me off I slowed down to let him get over he was just going too fast.

The motorcycle rider almost hit the cars parked on the street to the right of him. We all were traveling westbound on Hollywood Boulevard. The dude tried to get back in the far left lane when . . . BAM! His front tire hit the right rear panel bumper of an SUV. I don't know how he did that but that brotha flipped up, and over that SUV about twenty feet in the air. After that all I saw was a cloud of dust. I came to a complete stop for fear that I would run over him Sandy Bernard, and I got out of the car. Then I saw old dude walking towards us from out of the black smoke.

"Dude are you alright?" I asked.

"Na man I ain't" the motorcycle rider said.

He was wearing a black leather jacket which was all ripped up and shredded in the back. He had his helmet in his right hand it was all scratched up real bad. When the air cleared it looked like the bike was in a million pieces. I said to myself, "there's no way anybody should have walked away from that". A white van pulled up stopped then a dude opened the door and the biker dude climbed inside then closed the door then the van drove off. GOD was with him that's all I could say then all the other bikers pulled up shortly after looking for dude. A truck pulled up three people got out, and then started picking up pieces from the bike that were scattered all over the street.

They did not say a word to anyone It was like something out of the Twilight Zone movie. It was as if the crash never happened. Not one police car showed up I thought that was a little strange but I didn't trip so we got the hell up out of there. Things were becoming very clear to me at that point. I heard Mike's voice ring true in my head "Believe little of what you see, and very little of what you hear because shit happens . . . Are you with me?"

"What the hell happen back there? Did you see that shit CRASH! BAM! Dude come walking from out of that black smoke looking like The Terminator! Then he got in that van, and boned the hell out he's a lucky son-of-a— . . ." Bernard said.

"Watch your mouth man" Sandy said. "I hope he's alright he could be bleeding internally, and that's not good death may catch up with him later on down the road behind that wreck" Sandy said.

"It was an intervention he'll be all right maybe this will give him something to think about for the rest of his life. Life is something you don't play with, when you take life for granted it has a way of waking you up to reality very fast" I said to Sandy and Bernard.

The third page of my blue print was now complete. Bernard is the most important piece of my puzzle. I really couldn't say very much to Sandy or Bernard about my plan first I needed to finish my blue print. When everything was completely locked in place only then, I could reveal everything to Sandy and Bernard.

# PARLEY

It was a night of glamour a night to impress a night to really see what Hollywood was truly like up close and personal. Everyone would be at this industry party that is everybody who is actually somebody. They'll exit Limos in their most attention getting outfits good or bad. The wranglers would be there along with the star makers, and the star breakers. Everyone knows it wouldn't be a party without the sex, groupies, gold diggers, and the drugs. These elements have a complex position in this game. Sometimes we can get distracted by using those components thinking we can step up are game you have to stay focused.

This house was huge the driveway was large enough to have the entire block parked in it. This house looked like something out of the "Charleston Homes" magazine that features million dollar homes. The house looked like a castle with nice greenery around the outer parameter of a cobblestone horseshoe driveway. The house was beautifully landscaped with lights around the foundation that lit up the grounds to make its elegance visible from the street.

I parked the car, Bernard, Sandy and I exited it then headed towards the parity. All of these people were Bernard's close friends. They also knew Sandy through her mother that was a good thing but they didn't know me. So I had to be smooth in stealth like mode, and take notes. It was time for me to turn on the charm, and then let it do what it do. It was a quiet peaceful night the only thing you could hear was the sound of crickets, as we walked towards the house. As we got closer you could hear the muffled sound of music. Bernard opened the door, and the music rushed out from inside the house like someone pushed a booster button on the sound system.

Sandy and I walked in behind Bernard who was greeted by Gerald Flemings a flaming queen with blond hair blue eyes, chubby red cheeks, and very cheerful. He was about 5'7" He wore a black fedora; a white tux shirt that was partially tucked into his blue jeans. To complete his fashion statement he sported some brand new HI top white K-Swiss.

Gerald knows everybody's business that has something juicy going on in this world of illusion. Everybody wore his or her game face that night.

"Oh my God! It's Bernard! Hey everybody Mr. Jenkins is in the house! Hey! And who is this fine hunk standing next to you?" Gerald asked.

"Dude! This is my homeboy Jonathan Paul and his girl Sandy ya'll just Parleying up in here Hun?" Bernard said.

"Oh I know who she is! That's Connie daughter. Umm glad you could you could make it Sandy. So you're Jonathan Paul. Oooo stop! Baby, you are going to kill all in Hollywood with your look, and those eyes oh—my-GOD! Well just don't stand there come on in, and enjoy the party" Gerald said.

As Sandy and I walk into the party Gerald pull's Bernard to the side. It was cool I didn't trip because that was Bernard folks.

"Hey sweetness, Oh I love him I want him to be my baby's Daddy. What are the chances of you hookin' me up with him? That's your boy and everything right?" Gerald said.

Bernard politely leaned into Gerald's ear talking in a confidential manner.

"Check this out Homie that brotha there he's all about the Poo-na-na so don't get it twisted. You see that girl hanging on his arm? Look at that body. That's what he's about, so don't do anything stupid. Just back off G chill. It ain't that kind of party Dog you know how we do it. So stop playing man! Where's the weed at G?" Bernard said.

Bernard casually walked over to me. He needed to check out something that can be beneficial to his work.

"Jonathan, check this out smoke on this with your Girl-Doog. I'm gonna slide upstairs with Gerald for a moment. We're working on this show together, dude he's a wizard with that latex man. He just made up a new batch, and he claims it looks like real skin. I need to see this so you and my sista go Parley" Bernard said.

Sandy and I started walking in the direction of where the music was coming from. Bernard and Gerald walked over to a winding red oak staircase. It was beautifully designed with angels artistically placed between the top, and bottom rails of the black rod iron railing lead upwards to the second floor. As Bernard and Gerald slowly walked up the staircase,

Gerald peeked over the rails of the staircase checking me out like I was prime steak.

"Ok Brotha, I told you about my boy he doesn't get down like that. So don't mess with him you don't wanna see that side of him, it ain't nothing nice" Bernard said.

"Wow that's too bad Ok, since he's happy with the kitty cat I'll keep that in mind. I apologize for the way I acted, can you forgive me? I don't know what to do with myself at times. When those hormones flare up Oooo wee I just can't help myself but I'll be nice from now on" Gerald said.

I knew Gerald had a crush on me but that was OK. I was not gonna even waste my time trippin on that shit, but I could use him in my plans. Everything is working out fine and it was nice to know that Gerald worked with Bernard hum, an asset to my blue print. I looked over at Gerald as he walked upstairs with Bernard. I saw Gerald give me that "oh shit all we can be is friends" look but it was all good.

Gerald's house was beautiful. When you walked through the front door leading to the living-room there on the floor was this bone white unfinished granite tile. Clean white walls trimmed in red oak wood vaulted ceilings. The floor in the den was made of red cherry oak wood with pan cake steps leading down to a sunken den. A fire place that covers the whole wall with multi-colored slate that gave it that retro 70's look. His kitchen had a ranch style feel to it. The floor plan was open, and it had an Island in the center of the floor where meals were prepared It look like something out of your modern home magazines. The kitchen had black granite tile on the counter tops. The cabinets were chestnut red with small recessed lighting in the ceiling to give the kitchen a bright clean ever so perfect look. The brother had good taste. His back yard was a chef's dream with a horseshoe shaped barbeque pit with piggyback cookers on top to smoke meat. It had a grill just for cooking burgers, hot dogs or whatever else you want to get down with. His twenty-foot pool and Jacuzzi shared a rocky waterfall that flowed into the pool. A wall of palm trees incased the yard, and complimented its beautiful private landscape. Soft lights along a red cobblestone path way lead around the pool, and back to the house. It had that "Hawaiian" feel to it Gerald's house was laid. People were everywhere; sitting by the pool, in the pool, and dancing around the pool. The DJ took the mic and then said, "Ok, I want to slow it down a bit for the lovers in the house. It's a Supreme thing, let me introduce you to one of our newest members, Jonathan Paul where you at man?" DJ said.

"The DJ is calling your name Jonathan! Come on let's see what's going on outside" Sandy said.

When it rains it pours, in the back yard all the big wigs that were in the audition today were all here. The president Peter Zantex and his vice president Tony Hayden of Supreme studios had big smiles on their faces. I looked to the right of me and standing there was Michael talking on his phone as usual. Sandy and I walked out to the back yard. Connie walked up to me, and then led me to the edge of the pool. All eyes were on me. I was caught totally off guard Sandy, and Bernard knew all along how this was going to play out.

"I wanna thank everyone for being here at the last minute. Most of the times, as you well know things are planned in advance. We have added a new member to our family. Let me tell you those of you that know me know that when I cast for a part in a movie, I'm a very hard person to please. It's business, and it's about making MONEY. I don't wanna give a big speech but when I got the call about this young man, I had to meet him. I heard so many good things about him. Michael Zantex Peter's brother told me, you need to put him in one of your movies; he's going to be a big star you need to check him out. Well, I believe in giving people a chance so with no further a-do, Jonathan . . . welcome aboard" Connie said.

A guy walked up to Connie gave her an envelope then left. I saw Bernard and Gerald step out of the house through a sliding glass door. They walked towards Sandy, and stood next to her. Michael was right if they like you they will give you the world. Connie took my hand then placed an envelope in it. I open it and saw a black credit card and a checkbook. I peeked at the check book and saw a receipt in an account with my name on it for 55,000,000 dollars, and three sets of keys. One set looked like house keys the other two keys were to a Lincoln Navigator, and a Porsche. I was like cool . . . I acted like I was accepting an award from the Academy, and trust me I was nervous.

"I wanna first thank my Lord Jesus Christ for hearing my prayers. I asked Him to guide me and let me see my dream unfold in this business I love so much. Ever since my childhood I told people that I was going to be a big star one-day. I will not let anyone here at Supreme studios down.

Everything I touch will turn to gold. With my new family here at Supreme were going to do some big things, and thank you thank you all" I said.

Connie walked over to where the president Peter Zantex of Supreme studios was sitting. Wow when it rains it pours. When Peter and Connie got married she kept her maiden name to work under. That's why I couldn't make the connection between her and Peter it was all becoming crystal clear to me what was really going on. They've been play the game all this time as well, dam ain't that something Peter and Mike were brothers. Connie smiled at Peter He smiled back at her then she returned the smile to me.

"Have they set the date for the wedding?" Peter asked.

"I'll know by Wednesday then we can start sending out wedding invitations to all the studios, it's all coming together" Connie said.

"We start shooting in three weeks this event needs to take place soon. I do not want anything to stop production. I wanna make our little girl happy. If she's happy then were happy, all the way to the bank" Peter said.

Connie reached out her arms with the palms of her hands faced up to the heavens. She began clapping her hands as everyone else clapped along with her. It was a Mystical moment Sandy walked up to me and planted a warm juicy kiss on my lips then whispered in my ear, "I wanna show you something . . . we're done here"

"You two knew about this, and you didn't tell me!" I said.

"I wanted to surprise you. From this moment forward our lives will be filled with wonderful surprises" Sandy said.

"What are you telling me Sandy? I don't wanna play any games I know we just met today and all, but when I saw you I knew right away you were gonna be my wife. In you I see someone who will love me for me. GOD told me you're going to be my wife" I said.

I started looking around the yard as if I were looking for someone. I noticed a lady sitting under a palm tree she open a beautiful jewelry box on her lap reached inside it, and pulled out a little black box. She motioned for me to come to her. I walked over to the lady she took the little black box and then handed it to me.

"Don't worry it fits" the mystery woman said.

"Thank you" I replied.

The woman wore a green low cut Armani evening gown trimmed in diamond studs. She looked good for being in her, I'd say early eighties she had a sweet angelic demeanor about her as she smiled at me.

"Hurry up before she changes her mind Parley my son" the woman said.

I quickly walked back to where Sandy was standing. I took her left hand, and held it with my left hand. I looked deep into her eyes I knelt down on one knee. I then looked up into her beautiful angelic face. Suddenly tears begin to roll down her soft tender Rosie cheeks. Everyone in the house came outside to witness my proposal to Connie daughter.

"Sandy, I know we just met. But if you let me be the man of your dreams, you will make me the happiest man in the world. Will you marry me?" I asked.

"Yes, I'll marry you Jonathan" Sandy replied.

I slid a platinum 6-carat diamond engagement ring on to her finger then I stood up as she looked at her ring. We both hugged each other as laughter, and applause filled the air.

"Come on I wanna show you something" Sandy said.

Sandy took me by the hand to lead me to the surprise she had for me. Bernard stepped in front of me, and I stopped to talk with him. I looked around slightly distracted by his antics, and heard a voice softly calling my name. I turned looked over my left shoulder, and I saw the lady who had given me the ring. She was standing by a palm tree looking at me with a big smile on her face. Suddenly the woman's image turned into that of my own mother, and then she vanished into thin air . . .

"Dog, Hey Dog you can't drive all three of them vehicles at the same time. Why don't you let your roomie sport that jag? Bernard said.

I reached into my pocket pulled out my key ring. I removed the car key, and the town house key then gave it to Bernard.

"I'll be by this week to pick up my cloths, and personal things" I said.

Sandy pulled me by the arm leading me through the house then through the front door leaving the party. We both ran over to a long black four door stretch limousine. She opened the door pushed me inside then jumped in behind me. Sandy closed the door, and the driver slowly drove away.

"What are you doing? This limo belongs to somebody we can't be doing this . . ." I said.

"We can do this it's your limo from now on. You will use this car to go wherever you want to go. Your driver's name is Buddy. So kick back baby enjoy the ride, now you about to live the good life" Sandy said.

It seemed as though my new family was emerging slightly faster than I was. I was beginning to feel little afraid because success was unfolding a little bit too fast for me, something I didn't expect. But it was time for me to strap myself in, and hold on for dear life because this ride was about to get real bumpy. If you believe in the dreams you wish for it will soon manifest itself. But you must be ready to deal with what it has to offer you, with no questions ask. You have to want it just that bad, where you can taste it. Pray on it, make a plan, and then make it happen. Jesus said Knock, and the door will be opened unto you. Just be ready when that door opens.

# Heaven on Earth

Sandy reached up, and took a champagne bottle from a rack above her head. Then took two champagne glasses from a rack next to the door with her free hand. Sandy then reached into an ice chest, and took two pieces of ice from it. One by one she slowly dropped the ice cubes in to the glasses. I was really feeling this now, the uncertain feeling I had earlier was gone. I was in total control of this whole situation and I knew that I must remain focused. All of the studio executive's eyes were all on me this evening. I couldn't slip up, and give up my position. It was looking pretty damn good about now it was all coming together. Soon I would be one of Hollywood's newest up and coming star.

I looked at Sandy, and then thanked God for putting her in my life. I was not going to mess this up. We had to get married soon, and I was not going to play around with her. This was the woman for me, and the mother of my children. Sandy is so beautiful I love the way the moon shines on her hair, as it casts a dim shadow on her face while her hair blows in the wind. As her body slightly turned towards me I looked down at her thick caramel thighs. Her dress slightly shifted to fit her perfectly shaped body. As I leaned in to kiss the side of her neck, the scent of sweet honeysuckle perfume teased my male endorphins it drove me crazy. We became one in the back seat of the limo as we passionately kissed one another. Sandy handed me a glass she poured campaign into it then poured a glass for herself.

"A toast to us. May we have a long beautiful happy life together, with two beautiful children" Sandy said.

"Just two? Is that it?" I said.

"For now two is fine. Perhaps later on when you slowdown in your career, we can work on some more babies . . . deal? Jonathan, you have your work cut out for you" Sandy said.

Sandy leaned in, and gave me a sinful long kiss on the lips. Then she dipped her index finger into the champagne glass, and then placed it in her mouth. It was so sexy the way she sucked on her finger as if it was coated with cotton candy all the while giving me a seductive look.

"Deal . . . I have worked hard my whole life to get here. But no one believed in me. So, I ask God to show me what I needed to do. Finally I heard Him say "Make a plan, and then I'll take it from there," after that I met you. I asked him to send me someone and here you are. Wow we did the Hollywood party, got engaged all in one day. I'm finding out a lot about you, you're sneaky!" I said. "What do you mean? 'I'm Sneaky?" Sandy said.

"You knew about this whole thing. You and Bernard I should have known something was up with him when he started with you about that girlfriend stuff. I have to admit you got me" I said.

I looked out of the window of the limo as we cruised down Gerald's driveway. The soft dim lights aligned along the curb reminded me of when I was a little boy. One night my mother took me to a place called The Pike in San Diego. I remember hearing her refer to it as P.O.P. It was on a beautiful clear night my Mother, and I took a ride in a little boat. We glided down a river it was an island like setting, and there were lights on the ground. All I can remember was that they had this soft beautiful glow to them they were slightly hidden among the shrubbery along the banks of this canal.

As we drifted down the little river bank I could hear the sound of a macaw calling out in the night. I knew I was safe in my mother's arms. Then I heard elephants sounding off their trumpets, and then the powerful roar of a lion as it claimed its territory. I snuggled close to my mother as I held on tight peeking from the side of her breast, hoping that nothing would jumped out to get me. But I knew I was safe nestled under her arms. The lights were so picturesque the soft pink, green and amber lights just like the ones I'm looking at right now. They lead to the front gate. Slowly two large black metal gates began to open as the limo turned right on to Beverly Glenn gliding towards Sunset Boulevard. We stopped at a red light then it turned green the driver made a left turn on to Sunset heading back towards Hollywood.

We came to a street called Crescent Height's. The driver turned left then headed north. The road began to curve slightly we came to a street called Mount Olympus then stopped. The driver made a sharp right turn followed by a quick left turn we then proceeded up a hill. As I looked out of the window I saw tall slender trees planted in rows along the hillside. We climbed to the top of the hill, and then came to a street called Hercules just then Sandy took a handkerchief from the wine rack, and then blindfolded me. The driver stopped looked at Sandy though the rear view mirror Sandy nodded her head, and then the driver proceeded slowly towards a large two story white Italian Villa. It was surrounded with palm trees in the front yard. With a horseshoe cobblestone drive way that complemented the front view of the house. On the side of the drive way were eight rounded steps with lights under each riser leading to the front door. The driver pulled into the driveway and pushed a button on an intercom.

"Paul residence can I help you?" said a voice through the intercom. "Sandy what's going on?" I asked

"Man would you open the gate and stop playing" Sandy said.

"Where are we Sandy?" I said.

"The gate swung open, and the driver pulled into the drive way then stopped. Buddy our driver got out of the car walked around to the rear on my side, and opened the door. I got out of the limo with Sandy then Buddy closed the door.

"Buddy you can take the rest of the night off. If you get a call from Mr. Paul or me it won't be until tomorrow sometime around 9:00 am" Sandy said.

Buddy was a female limo driver. She was a dark skin thin lady with a mannish way about her. She had a very confident spirit with a hip-type personality. She stood about 4'11" weighed no more than 90 pounds. She wore a black suit with black shoes to match wearing a black limo cap that was tilted to the side. She looked like one of the boys. I tried to take the blindfold off but Sandy stopped me. "What are you doing? You can't look yet . . ." Sandy said.

"It ain't nothing Just hit me on the hip. I got you don't trip, if you need me I'm here" Buddy said.

"Alright then Buddy we'll see tomorrow, you be safe" I said.

Sandy took off the blindfold and oh my God, I thought I was in heaven. As I looked around at the beauty that surrounded me I couldn't believe my eyes. Buddy got into the limo backed up passing the white gate's, they kind of remind me of the White Pearly Gates that was referred to in the Bible. The front yard resembled just that of a garden sanctuary for the Gods. In the yard there were two six foot white marble stone carved statues of Goddess posing in real life form. Truly this was Heaven on earth; I wished my mother could see this.

Sandy led me through a huge red oak double door it was the front entrance to this beautiful home. We stepped into a huge foyer with two sets of stairs that ran alongside each wall to the left and to my right was a staircase that lead directly up to the second floor. On the floor in the foyer was this Cold black marble tiled walk way that lead down three flights of steps to the living room. On my right under the staircase I could see downtown Los Angeles through a large picture window. The living room floor was a Cream toffee plush carpet. It had a huge fireplace in the center of the room, and a seven piece sectional sofa with mixed throw pillows perfectly on the sofa near the picture window.

A large 72" 1080p flat screen TV that popped up from out of the floor complete with a Bose surround sound theater system. Down three more flights of steps was a 25'x19' dining room. With a 14 piece dining room set a Cristal chandelier that hung in the center of the room. It had a ranch style kitchen complete with a seven foot Island in the center. The walls were filled with honey maple oak cabinets complete with glass, and laced in gold leaf. The kitchen had a double stainless steel sink a double stacked oven, and a 14'x12' walk-in refrigerator.

Over the Island hung an old fashioned copper ductless vent with six electric burners on the counter. Over the counter hung a pot rack overhead and a stainless steel dishwasher to the left of the sink. We walked out of the kitchen to the back of the house through a 60"x80" sliding glass seamless door. I saw the entire San Fernando Valley it was breath taking. The back yard looked like something from out of Caesars Palace. I saw ficus, palm, banana and cherry trees. In the center of all that beauty was a 20' Olympic size swimming pool. It had a baby blue bottom a Jacuzzi with a waterfall, and more white marble carved statues of Olympian Goddess's. They were all aliened on both side of the pool Sandy stood behind me pressed against my back with her arms wrapped around me. "What do you think?" Sandy said.

"What do I think? This Is Heaven on earth, I love it" I said.

"Complements of Supreme studios, it's all yours baby" Sandy said.

Sandy walks me over to the large picture window in the living room. I looked down at the side of the house and saw a brand new Black SUV Navigator and a Black 2010 Porsche with black tinted windows parked side by side in front of my new four-car garage "You're really goanna like this" Sandy said.

Sandy took me by the hand led me to a room across the way. She opened the door turned on the lights; it was a screening room and a 24 track digital recording system all in a 25'x20' room. Speakers were built inside the walls, plush theater chairs were arranged in a slanted downward slope facing a 100" flat screen 1080p TV, and it was built into the wall.

"Well what do you think? Was this part of your dream?" Sandy said. "Oh my God yes and more. I don't know what to say, I can see a lot of good projects jumping off from here" I said.

We left the room, and Sandy took me upstairs where there were five bedrooms. We walked down a hall towards a door at the end of the hallway. We entered a 25'x30' master bedroom suite. On a platform was a king sized bed with a black, and gold comforter with matching pillows on it. On the wall in front of the bed were four 32" flat screen televisions. On each side of the TV's the walls had been turned into a saltwater fish tanks where brightly colored fish swam all around.

I walked into the Master bathroom gold trimmed mirrors were everywhere. The floor was tiled in a white unfinished marble. The shower stall was tiled in small white 4"x4" marble blocks it was completed with a shower system that sprayed water from the top, and the sides. The casing around the shower was seamless the shower was just a step away from a 110"x5' hot tub. Two white marble pillars that were carved in the likeness of Hercules braced on top of the hot tub, as their shoulders held up the ceiling. The hot tub was tiled in the same manner as the shower stall. Between the pillars were three pancake style steps leading to the floor of the bathroom. To the back of the restroom were two black toilets trimmed in gold leaf, and next to it a his and hers seashell waterfall sinks man Caesar would have loved this bathroom. As I exited the bathroom I saw Sandy lying on the bed pointing a remote control towards the back of the bedroom.

"Open the drapes with this Jonathan" Sandy said.

I walked over to the bed Sandy handed me the remote. When I pressed the button the drapes glided across the wall. On the other side of this sliding glass door revealed a 10'x12' balcony. The view of the backyard was absolutely astonishing.

I walk over to the bed sat next to Sandy we snuggled as we look out into the back yard. I was so thankful for all that God had done for me. I knew that he would continue to do more for me in the future.

"It feels like we've known each other for ever. You make me feel good inside. The way I feel about you, is a way that I have never felt about anyone" I said.

"I feel the same way about you. Something happens to me when we kiss that has never happen with anybody. When you kissed me at Melodies today, you made me feel so warm inside. Something inside me told me that I belong to you and only you. I will do everything it takes to be a good wife to you Jonathan. I will also love you like I love myself and baby I will submit to all of your wishes" Sandy said.

"If that's the way you feel then we are on the same page, so this is what I want us to do. In three weeks I start working on Peter's project. And I think we should get married soon, what you say? Two weeks from now?" I said.

"What ever you want to do I'm all for it and you don't have to call mother Connie anymore she's your mom too. I'll talk to her tomorrow about our decision and by the end of this week it'll all be worked out . . . Who's your best man?" Sandy asked.

"That works for me, Bernard is my best man that's my Dog he's like my brother. I don't have family here in L.A. My mom died five years ago it's just me my aunt who lives in Texas, and my two brothers and one sister" I said.

"Well I'm your family now, I'm sorry to hear about what happened to your mom . . . I would have loved to have met her. I can tell you really loved her I can hear it in your voice. We'll send for your aunt a week before the wedding the girl's and I will go look at some dresses this weekend" Sandy said.

Sandy turned over to face me as she snuggled up against my chest looking at me with burning desire in her eyes. I wanted to talk to her about our relationship to set things right.

"Sandy, I want to talk to you about something. You're a gift from God, and I cherish my relationship with Him. I'm not perfect and I do know right from wrong. I don't wanna do anything to mess up what He has given me. What I'm trying to say is would you be mad if I told you I didn't want us to have sex until our wedding night? I want us to do this right I don't want anything hanging over our heads. I want us to have a clear conscience when we say 'I do'," I said. "That makes me respect you even more the fact that you ask, this lets me know how much you really care about me. I love you Jonathan Paul" Sandy said.

Sandy positioned herself in front of me facing the balcony, as we slept holding one another until the next morning when the sun came up.

# CHANGE OF PLANS

It was a beautiful morning I had just taken a refreshing dip in the pool. I was still taking everything in it was still hard to believe. I remember years ago when some friends and I drive around in this neighborhood. They all raved about how it would be a dream come true to live on top of Mount Olympus. I would just smile, and marvel at the beautiful homes as we cruised up and down the street. I knew back then that I would live on this hill some day. I kept that thought to myself as I listened to them sounding like little kids, as they fussed over the homes as we passed by them.

I remember when our parents would take us to the super market they would leave us in the car. We would play the car game the first good-looking car that passed by, you would try to beat them by saying "that's my car" before they would. Man those were happy times. Sandy had just finished making breakfast she strolled out of the back door with a tray of bacon, two eggs some toast, and a glass picture of orange juice mixed with champagne. I noticed she was wearing a yellow two-piece swimsuit she was looking very sexy this morning. She placed the tray on the table, and sat the orange juice next to it. Then fed me a piece of bacon.

"Good Morning sweetheart . . . did enjoy your swim?" Sandy Said.

"Yes, I did . . . I like that swimsuit you're wearing baby REAL NICE" I said.

"I went home this morning, and picked up a few things while you were sleeping. I didn't want to wake you, on my way back I stopped at the market, and got some groceries" Sandy said.

"You're so good to me I like that, what's your agenda for today?" I said.

"I wanna contact my girls and see if we can hook up this weekend to look at some dresses" Sandy said.

"Ok I have to meet with Benny at 10:00 this morning to go over some stunts we shoot in three days. Then I need to stop by my old apartment, and pick up some cloths, a few man things you know. Call Buddy; tell her to take the day off. I wanna take the Porsche out for a spin" I said.

"Well baby while your out doing your man thing I need to stop by Supreme to pick up your script. I got a text this morning from mother saying it was ready. After that mother and I will do lunch then I'll see you later. I think I'll go home tonight I need to clean my place up it's a mess" Sandy said.

Sandy picked up the glass picture of mimosa, poured me a glass handed it to me, and then poured a glass for herself. Sandy picked up the joint that Bernard gave me last night it was on the tray. She picked up a lighter from the trey, and lit the joint.

"I forgot all about that, where did you find it?" I said.

"It was on the sink in the bath room. This morning I called the maid service. She didn't need to see all that, so I just moved it. I knew you forgot it was in there. They'll clean your place twice a week, and I told them to send the same person my mother uses. She's very good, and you can trust her" Sandy said.

Sandy took a drag from the joint then passed it to me.

"That's cool I can get use to this, by the way who was that guy you were talking to last night that opened the front gate?" I said.

"That's the houseboy Justin he stays in the guesthouse in the back. He watches the place when you're not here, and does whatever you need him to do. He runs errands cooks, shops for groceries that kind of stuff you know" Sandy said.

I took two big drag on the joint, and then passed it to Sandy. At that moment Justin came walking up from the guesthouse.

Sandy leans over to whisper in my ear. "He's my half-brother his mother ran off with the gardener who was fifteen years younger than her. Justin was ten when she left oh, and he write's comic books," Sandy said as she begans to chuckle.

"And what wrong with that, you laughing?" I replied.

"We'll talk about it later (He, he) she looks down at Justin's feet with a smirk on her face" Sandy said.

Justin was about 6'3"220 pounds with an athletic build. He looked like a Greek God with caramel completion, and steel grey eyes. He had shoulder length black wavy hair perfect white teeth. He wore an Ed Hardy T-shirt with the sleeves rolled up. Justin was sporting the latest skinny jeans with some Old Navy flip flops. He just came back from getting his "Meddie Peddie" and gossiping about the latest Hollywood madness.

"Good morning!" Justin said.

"And good morning to you . . . Justin I want you to meet my fiancé Jonathan Paul. You missed our engagement party last night at Gerald's place! You should have been their It was a blast" Sandy said.

I heard all about it at the nail salon this morning. I also heard he's the newest FAMILY MEMBER at Supreme STARING in Peter's new film! WELL Congratulations JONATHAN" Justin said.

I could tell by the way Justin spoke he really didn't like me very much. Justin felt that he should have been the one to have the house and the career. He felt like he was on the outside looking in and that his talents had been overlooked. He too had dreams of being an actor and having the career but his step-dad Peter would never give him a shot. Peter thought Justin was not good enough because he didn't have the "Zantex blood" running through his veins.

"Nice to meet you Justin your sister tells me you write comic books. Sandy kicked me when I made reference about his comic book, but I played it off. That's cool have you had anything published yet?" I asked.

"No, but I have some things in the works. My buddy and I sent a demo over to Japan about a few weeks ago they're taking a look at it. I think we have a good chance of getting picked up" Justin said.

"You never told me that Justin that's good" Sandy said.

"I have a meeting with my agent this morning. I'm going to be out for a few hours, and I'll be back later to clean the pool. I just though I would let you know where I am going in case you needed me for anything," Justin said.

"It's cool, Do you thing man break a leg with your comic book. Sandy is trying so hard not to bust out laughing. We'll it's was nice meeting you Justin" I said.

Justin left through the side gate near the garage he stopped turned then called out to Sandy.

"SANDY! Can I see you for a moment?" he said.

"Aw shit here we go! I'll be right back" Sandy said. "Why you laughing what's so funny?" I said. "I'll tell you when I come back" Sandy replied.

Sandy walked over to Justin and they began talking.

"How long have you known this Jonathan character?" Justin asked.

"Not long why? What business is it of yours anyway?" Sandy said.

"I'm concerned that's why. You're my sister I want the best for you. Girl you don't even know this guy and you're talking about marrying him? What's up with that?" Justin said.

"You don't need to worry about me, I'm a big girl I know enough to know, that I want to be his wife he's good to me and I love him that's what's up Justin" Sandy said.

"YOU LOVE HIM? You don't know anything about him!" Justin said.

"Who in the hell are you raising you voice at? You're not my FATHER and you're DAMN sure not my man. What you need to do is get a life and stay the fuck up out of mine. You got that little brother?" Sandy said.

Sandy walked back over to me, and it was obvious she was pissed off at Justin. "Everything all right baby?" I said.

Justin exited the gate looked at me in a menacing way as he left the yard; he slammed the gate behind him.

"I needed to set him straight. He is always hatin on somebody'. He's been that way all of his life. He's never had anything good to say about anyone I've ever been involved with. So he can kiss my ass I know that much" Sandy said.

"Baby don't even trip a lot of people will have negative things to say about us. But that's cool because as long as we love each other that's all that matters" I said.

"You're right I apologize for the way I carried on. He just piss'es me off with his bullshit" Sandy said.

"For a moment I had the feeling he did didn't like me very much" I said.

"That bastard doesn't like anybody that's just the way he is. When you get to know him you'll understand what I'm talking about. He's been that way all his life, messed up in the head" Sandy said.

Just then I received a call from Benny there was a death in his family he had to leave the country to bury his father. He also gave me heads up about the shoot with Quawn Lee; he pulled out of the show.

"Jonathan call mike and tell him there has been a change of plans. My dad passed away today, and I need go home to be with my family. Plus the show has been canceled when they find a replacement for Lee the studio will contact you. When that happens we can continue working on your fight scenes" Benny said.

"Hey man, I'm sorry to hear about your father. Is there anything you want me to do for you?" I said.

"I'm good Bro. I just need to get my head together and be with my family I'll be in touch" Benny said.

"Alright then keep your head up man. I'll say a prayer for you and the family" I said.

I hung up the phone then just stared at the pool.

"What wrong Jonathan?" Sandy said.

"That was Benny there has been a change of plans. His father just passed away today, and he has to leave the country to bury him. The studio cancelled the show because Lee backed out of the project. When they find a replacement the studio will call Mike" I said.

"That's too bad about Benny's dad you'll be fine it's not like your hurting for money. So don't trip baby it's a good thing. Well that means you and I can spend some time together before you start shooting on my dad's project" Sandy said.

"You're right, I just feel bad for Benny. I know what he's going through right now. I miss both my parents I would give anything for them both be here with me now" I said.

Sandy hugged me then kissed me on the forehead.

"Baby, what was so damn funny to you when your brother walked up" I asked Sandy.

"First it was the weed making me laugh then when I looked down at Justin's feet, and saw his toe nails they were painted HOT PINK! I thought that shit was funny," Sandy said. "You know you're wrong for that. He can't help it that he likes PINK" I said.

We kissed I stood up with Sandy in my arms and walked over to the pool. I stepped down into the water with her in my arms we submerge under water with only our heads above the water kissing romantically. Then we slowly disappear under water.

# 1X-LOVER

I'm loving this car already it rides so smooth and handles the road like butter. As I ride by other cars it's as though they are standing still. I'm only doing forty miles an hour just a little bit over the speed limit; I thought I'd better slow this boxer down before LA's finest pull me over. I wanted to stop by Mike's office to let him see my new toy. It was early yet and there was hardly anyone on Ventura Boulevard that was strange. I needed to get some gas I was almost on E. I hate it when my gas needle goes below half tank. I pulled into a gas station and who do I see? Darnell White an old high school classmate of mine. He was the class clown in my drama class who always got in trouble because of his mouth. My classmates and I nick named him "Dirty White" because he always wore dirty cloths to school.

"Jonathan Paul! How the hell are you man? I like this ride! Man long time no see. What are you doing now selling drugs? Pimping? You can tell me," Darnell said.

"Man it ain't like that Dog I work in the movie business" I said.

"Get the fuck outta here! You work in the movies business?" Darnell said.

"Yea that's me man all day long. What's up with you Dog?" I said.

"I run this gas station for my dad. We do all right, I work here three days a week on Thursdays and Fridays I work at a school teaching drama to seventh graders" Darnell said.

"Right, right but you're still in the mix dog. That's cool you're working with kids man, God's gonna bless you for what you're doing believe that. Hey look I don't live that far from here now that I know you're here, I'll buy my gas from you from time to time when I'm in the area alright?" I said.

"Don't get out man I'll pump the gas for you. It's really good to see you Jonathan. I remember when we were in school you said you were going to work in the movie business. Everybody laughed at you; I'd like to see their faces now. Ok man your good to go. It was really nice to see you. Maybe one day when you're not to busy you can come by the school talk to my kids about the movies business. I work at Burbank High School you know where that is right?" Darnell said.

"Yea, I know where it is my Ninja. Here's my number call me some times. Hey ah look, I'm working on some things you might be interested in. It's legitimate just call me, I'll come through, and check you out . . . How much do I owe you for the gas Dog?" I said.

"Your money is no good at this station. Man come on, It's cool you're good, I'll see you around" Darnell said.

"Darnell White . . . Thanks man I'll be talking with you" I said.

Mike's office is about ten minutes away from Darnell's father's gas station. As I zoomed down Ventura Boulevard bumping my sounds, I got a call from Jasmine. "Hello" I said.

"JONATHAN! Please help me! I'm scared my ex is trying to kick the door in" Jasmine replied fear in her voice.

"He's what? How did he find you? I said.

"My Aunt told him . . . AHHHHH! He's got a gun. No, Baby, no, no, NO!" Jasmine screamed.

My phone dropped the call I pressed redial Jasmine's phone went to voice mail. I threw the phone in the passenger seat down shifted to first turned around in the middle of the street, and took off like a bat out of hell. I jumped on the 405 north ripping through traffic weaving in and out like a mad man. It was almost as if time had stood still and I was the only person on the highway. My phone started beeping it was a voice message. I ignored it as I flew down the highway. Soon I was on the Hollywood Freeway In no time I pulled up in front of my old spot. I saw this dude running to his car he was dressed in a white jogging suit it had blood all down the front of it. I took a real good look at him as he jumped into a Grey 300 Charger. He started the engine then mashed out almost hitting two parked cars. His license plate read: 1X-LOVER. I rushed over to the opened front gate, and then ran up the stairs in front of the building. I open the door and heard people screaming. The elevators were not in service so I ran up to the third floor using the stairs. All of the neighbors that lived on my floor were all standing in the hallway screaming frantically.

I ran towards Jasmines front door which was blown off its hinges. I stepped inside of Jasmine's living room it looked like hurricane Evelyn just hit. Blood was everywhere. I looked around but couldn't find Jasmine. I made my way to her bedroom, and found her stretched out naked on her bed. She had a bullet hole in the center of her forehead and carved in her breast was "1X-LOVER". The nine-millimeter that was used on Jasmine was lying on the floor next to the bed. Stuffed in her mouth was a note that read "This little birdie won't be singing any more" Suddenly Bernard entered the room. "Jonathan, what did you do? Man, don't touch anything" he said.

"She called me on my cell phone, she needed my help. She screamed, and then the phone went dead. Man I got over here as FAST! As I could . . . I found her like this, and then you showed up" I said.

"I'm calling 911 . . . Hello there's been a murder . . . Jonathan what's the address here?" Bernard asked.

Bernard handed the phone to me.

"7734 South Sycamore apartment 202," I said.

"Ok, Sir some officers will be there soon are you alright?" asked the operator.

"I'm fine . . . Ok ma'am the officers are here" I said.

Four police officers entered the room with their guns drawn. They asked Bernard, and I to leave the room. Six other CSI homicide detectives entered the apartment four of them went into the room with Jasmine. The other two CSI detectives stayed in the living room with Bernard, and me. One detective looked around the living room, and the other one talked with me for hours. We ended up at the police station. Later Sandy, Connie and Peter walked in to the CSI detective office looking for me. "JONATHAN! What's going on? When you called we came as soon as we could" Sandy said.

"There was a murder next door to my old apartment. It was someone I use to talk to. I was on my way to see Mike when I got a call from Jasmine. She said her ex had just kicked in her door She was screaming, for me to help her. When I got to the apartment she was dead" I said. "Are you alright baby?" Sandy said.

"I'm fine, I was just too late. If I hadn't gone to the gas station maybe, she'd still be alive" I said.

"Look, shit happens. Sometimes we have no control over things like that. You did what you could!" Connie said.

"It's all over the news; don't worry Jonathan we'll get you the best lawyers to deal with this madness. Did you touch anything in the apartment?" Peter asked.

"No, I was too shocked to do anything Bernard called 911for me . . ." I explained.

"If I were in the same situation I wound have done the very same thing you did. You were trying to save a life, I believe you meant well. It's going to be all right, they 'ell find her killer" Sandy said.

Just then detective Stone walked up. He was wearing a blue long sleeve shirt with a red tie. On the side of his waist revealed his badge, and a 45 strapped to his right thigh. He wore black pants and a pair of black soft-soled shoes. Sandy was talking to me as detective Stone waited until she was finished before directing his question to me. He had a plastic bag with the murder weapon in it, and a note they found in Jasmine's mouth. The detective showed me a picture of Jasmine and a man standing together. "Was this the man you saw leaving the building?" Detective Stone asked. "Yea . . . That's him" I said.

"Do you remember what he was wearing?" Detective asked.

"He was wearing a white jogging suit. It had blood all down the front of it . . . I was able to get this as he drove off" I answered.

I wrote down the license plate for the detective on a sheet of paper, and then put it in a folder that read "1X-LOVER CASE".

"1X-LOVER . . . I saw that car today when I was leaving the cleaners on Santa Monica Boulevard. I have everything I need from you. Now if I need to talk to you how can I reach you?" Detective Stone asked.

I wrote my address and phone number on Detective Stone's folder, he looked at me in a strange way. He told me that he recognized me from a movie he once saw this past weekend.

"You're the actor that was in that movie with Rasmondo Asonte. The name of that movie was? Wait a minute THE LATIN KINGS . . . you play the role of a musician. I loved what you told Rasmondo in that one scene, you were trying to get on the stage to play with Osco Pointe "He called me to the stage not you're punk ass". That was funny. I guess you told him a thing or two look, I'll call you when we get more information regarding this case, thanks for coming in I'll be talking with you" Detective Stone said.

Detective Stone left the office. I sat down in a chair, and began blaming myself for Jasmines death. I mentally beat myself up because I couldn't get there in time to help her. I felt like I let her down. Just the other night I told her I would always protect her.

"I can still hear Jasmine's voice in my head. I can't imagine the horror of being trapped, not being able to get away to save your own life. Seeing her life flash in front of her face. I see her desperately reaching out for me to rescue her from that monster. As she stared down the barrel of his cold, blue steel nine-millimeter she knew that her time was up. I COULD HEAR IT IN HER VOICE!" I said out loud.

You can't blame yourself for what happened to her. This guy will pay for what he has done. You have to move on with your life now Son. I'm sure the guys here will take care of this matter. You can't go on beating yourself up over this. You have to stay focused let them do their job, there's nothing more you can do," Peter said.

I got up from the seat Connie hugged me to let me know that her family had my back. My first impression of Connie was that she was all business, and just a total bitch. I thought she couldn't separate work from home, but who knew that her look would soon turn into a reassuring one.

"It's over now I don't want to sound cold or calloused, but you need to get your head back in the game. We start production in three weeks. So you need to be over with this by the time we start shooting. Do you understand what I'm saying Jonathan? "Connie asked. "Yes ma'am I understand . . . the show must go on" I replied.

We went outside, and man Sandy was holding my hand so tight it was almost as if she thought I was going to leave her. Her feelings towards me had not changed. Though I thought she would flip behind this whole ordeal. My guilty conscience ate me up knowing Jasmine, and I where together a few days before her death. I felt Sandy was goanna back out of the relationship I didn't' think she would understand". I had to keep a level head and stay focused with my plan.

"Mom, the girls and I are going to look at dresses this weekend. I'd like for you to go with us so you and I can sit with the wedding planner to get some ideas. Jonathan and I want to get married two weeks from today" Sandy said.

Peter and Connie smiled when they heard the news. Beginning tomorrow Peter would start making phone call to all the magazines and studios. To let them all know his little girl was getting married to Hollywood's newest star Jonathan Paul.

# VOICE MESSAGE

I found Sandy's parents to be really sophisticated. I knew there would be days when we would lock horns, but I was confident that it would all soon pass. I could tell by the way Connie talked to me at the police station she's was a pepper, and she don't take no shit from anybody. That's what I liked about her she was tactful in way she spoke to me. But she has a way of getting her point across to you. Now I know what Sandy meant when she said "what Connie wants Connie gets".

Sandy's father was cooler than shit. My father was never open-minded enough where I could feel comfortable chillin and talking with him. He was in US navy a true military man real old school and stern. I couldn't express myself with him, with my father Bob Livingston it was "do as I say and shut the FUCK up or I'm goanna beat your ass" kind of guy. Seemed like I got my ass beat all the time. I can still see the look on his face when he would beat me. I felt as though he hated me, but most of the time he was never at home always out to sea. When he was home it was like he wasn't there at all. We never talked about school my career or things I would have liked to have done with him. Mr. Livingston was a cold piece of work.

My siblings were so afraid of that man that even at his gravesite all four of us waited to see him be put into the ground. When the bulldozer dropped dirt into his grave. In anticipation I wanted to see that hole filled with dirt, covered all the way up. My mother didn't even go to the gravesite; I guess she hated him that much for whatever reason. To this day that still plays in my head. We had closure on that day when the last speck of dirt was spread over his grave. We all knew at that moment that he was REALLY gone, and that Bob Livingston could never ever in this life hurt us again.

Sandy's parents got into their car and left. They were going to the studio to tie up some loose ends regarding the project. Later go to Yamashiro's for another meeting with investors regarding the project. I needed to go somewhere to clear my head. I didn't want to go by myself and I knew Sandy wanted to ride in the new Porsche. So I drove out to Venice Beach were the two of us just chilled.

I parked in the Venice Beach parking lot near the tennis courts we both got out of the car. I heard my phone beeping I picked it up looked at it and noticed that it had a voice message. I laid it back down on the seat. I thought it would wait so I locked the car Sandy and I walked towards the boardwalk holding hands. People were everywhere walking up and down the boardwalk it reminded me of The Pike, but without the rides. There where food courts to the right and as far as the eye see. People were riding their bikes up and down the boardwalk walking their dogs, and others were just chillin' like the two of us.

There was a shabby looking white dude sitting on a trash can. He was holding up a sing that said "I'm not going to lie to you I need donations for weed" Sandy and I found that very amusing. Shit you'll almost see anything on Venice Beach. We took in the fresh breeze of the ocean as the mist danced upon our faces. It was soothing to my soul to stroll on the beach watching the sparking blue and green shimmers of light flicker in the ocean. As the sun set it was just the medication I needed to put me back on point, and back in the game.

Sandy and I rolled up our pant legs then we walked out into the water as far as we could before we got all wet. The cool salt water rushed past our feet, and then slowly ran back out to sea it was very refreshing. My Mother use to say, "When you let the water rush onto your feet, it cleans your body of all bad sprits. You say a prayer then all the negative spirit will wash away, and cast themselves back out into the sea forever.

"What are you thinking about right now?" Sandy asked.

"When my mother and I would spend hours at the beach. I would play in the sand digging for sand crabs. She would tell me to stand by her just like you and I are doing right now" I answered.

"You miss your mother don't you?" Sandy said.

"Yes I do" . . . Standing here with you reminds me of when she and I would let the water hit are feet. The water between my toes the sand moving underneath my feet felt so good. I was a little dude and I would hold on tight to her leg trying to keep my balance. She would say, "Whenever you feel down and out come to the ocean let her wash your feet like Jesus washed his disciple's feet, and then you'll be just fine" I said.

"I believe that, I feel at peace here with you right now. Wow you REALLY loved your mother, that's a good thing. I know you will love me just like you loved her. I understand the love you had for her is different . . . I remember on my sixteenth birthday my mother told me to watch how a man treats his mother. If he's good to her he'll be good to you" Sandy said.

At that moment a cold chill shot through my body. I reached for Sandy held her in my arms ever so tightly. She held me in the same way. Suddenly I heard a voice in my head it told me "love, and cherish this gift I give to you. Let no man come between the two of you. She is your rib, and you are hers. Be good to one another". I picked Sandy up in my arms carried her to a more dryer area in the sand. Gently I laid her down in the sand then gave her a long passionate kiss on her hot red juicy lips.

I ran my fingers through her hair as she looked at me with those beautiful bluish green eyes. At that moment a lady walked up to us and wanted to take our picture. She was an elderly lady dressed like a tourist wearing a white straw hat. Her face was very pleasant looking, she kind of reminded me of a farmer's wife. Wearing a white summer dress and white sandals to go with her outfit. In her right hand was a digital camera then over her left shoulder hung a white oversized beach bag.

"Excuse me I couldn't help but notice the two of you out there at the beach. You looked so adorable holding her in your arms you two remind me of my husband and I when we first got married. We were so in love with each other back then. He's gone home now, so I take pictures here on the beach to pass the time away kind of like a hobby you know . . . May I?" The elderly woman asked.

When she started to take our picture her cell phone rang; the woman reached into her white bag looking for her phone but couldn't find it. She could hear it ringing finally after taking almost everything out of her bag she finds her phone.

"Oh shoot! I can never find anything in this old bag of mine . . . Oh well it stopped ringing it went to voice message, I'll check it later. I know who it was just my grandson he worries about me out here on the beach. I always tell him "I'm fine I can take care of myself". Where were we? Oh yes can you pick her up like you did when you two were on the beach? That's it!" The elderly lady said.

She took a lot's of pictures of Sandy, and I that day. I have a feeling they are going to look real nice. I noticed she had this very intense look on her face while she took our picture.

"Son, when I get to my beach house I can upload these pictures to my computer then print them out just like LA Print Shop does. If you give me your e-mail address I can send you the pictures. I see my camera like's you, both of you photograph well . . . you know I live on the boardwalk in a beach house next to Winkie Dogs down the way. My husband bought it for me 16 years ago. Just last year he passed my grandson, and his wife runs the Hot dog stand for me. Now I'm just enjoying my life for a change. I just love it out here I meet so many interesting people like you two. I'm sorry; I'm just going on and on! Here write your information in this tablet," the elderly woman said.

She was a sweet little old lady before she left she gave two coupons to Sandy for us to eat at Winkie dogs. She reminded me of my fifth grade teacher Mrs. Blanched. That lady would talk your head off she kind of looked a little bit like her too. After I wrote my e-mail address in her tablet the woman walked off towards the weight pen, and then disappeared into the crowed. Sandy and I continued walking on the boardwalk and looking at the side walk art that people were making.

We saw a guy sitting on the ground with all types of different colors of spray paint. We watched as he sprayed red and yellow paint on white canvas-type cardboard. He took a putty knife made some squiggles on the paper then took some newspaper, and smeared it across the canvas. When he was done it looked like water in the ocean. After that he sprayed once more with a can of blue spray paint with the same knife he etched what looked like a boat into the paint.

Once again he sprayed the canvas with a can of white paint, and repeated the process. It looked like the moon had cast its reflection on the boat it was unbelievable. When he was done it looked like something from a dream with two moons and sparkling stars. And the ocean with a boat sailing across the open sea in outer space. We waited until it dried. I gave the man twenty five dollars after he framed the picture I gave it to Sandy, she was so happy. I love to see her smile her whole face just lights up like a kid in a candy store. By that time it was getting dark the sidewalk venders were packing it in for the day. So we stopped off by Winkie Dogs, and used our coupons. We ordered chilly dogs two root beers then headed back to the car. As we sat in the car eating our hot dogs we watched the sun go down while listening to Sade.

My phone started beeping again Sandy reached behind her in the seat grabbed the phone then handed it to me. I went through the prompt system to retrieve the message that I had received. I listened to the first voice message. It was a call from a casting agency for a feature film I had auditioned for about two weeks ago. The second message was a call back saying they had changed their minds and that they wanted me to come by the studio to pick up a script tomorrow around at 10:00 a.m. at Cougar Studios. I couldn't just yet let anyone know what was going on just yet. I just signed with Supreme studios, and they couldn't know about this. It would be a breach of contract on my part if they found out, my plan was in motion. When I get home I needed to call Bernard because I was going to need him to help me work this magic.

I listened to the third voice message I heard a strange voice in the background then Jasmine screaming. Then I hear what sounded like someone being beaten and punched on then I hear "OH MY GOD! BABY NO, PLEASE DON'T DO THIS!! NO! NO! . . ."BANG"!

# IT'S ON

I pulled up into the driveway of my new home pressed the clicker on my sun visor to open the gate. I pulled into the driveway then parked. Sandy got out from the passenger side and met me on the steps. I opened the door with my keys Sandy walked in the house, I closed the door behind us and Sandy turn on the house lights from the foyer.

We went upstairs to the bedroom Sandy walked over to the liquor bar to make a green apple martini for us. It's on and crackin'. All she wants to do is just relax, and chill with her man tonight. "Are you okay? When you're done I'll be out here on the deck waiting for you" Sandy said.

"I'm fine I just need to call Bernard I need him to do something for me" I said.

"Baby, are you sure you're fine? After you checked your messages at the beach you seemed a little distant. We hardly talked to each other on the way home," Sandy said

"Everything is fine sweetheart. I need to do something very important. Trust me nothing's wrong, are you staying tonight? I really wish you would" I said.

"Yes baby I'm staying" She replied.

Sandy was beginning to sense that the message I had received wasn't pleasant. She was worried that I wouldn't do anything stupid I had a look on my face, she didn't like.

"Baby I don't want sound like I'm prying into your business but we are getting married in a few weeks, and I want us to start off trusting each other. I don't want to ever think you would hide anything from me or lie to me about anything you hear me? "Sandy said.

I picked up my drink looked at it then looked at Sandy. I had to let her know what happened at the beach with the voice message. The best way to do that was to let her hear it. She was right I had to trust her, if she's going to be my wife. I couldn't hide anything from her. So I took out my cell phone handed it to her so she could hear that last disturbing message.

"I just killed this two timing Snitch. I told her I would find her, and when I did she was a dead Bitch. It's, your entire fault! Don't nobody play me for a fool. Jonathan, that is your name right? Your next I'm coming for your ass, so just watch your back . . . That's all I can tell you . . ." said the voice.

"That's sick he wanted you to hear that girl being murdered? Something is wrong with this guy. Baby, who was that?" Sandy said.

"Jasmine's ex-fiancé all we did was go out for a bite to eat one time. This was before you and I got together. We ended up back at my place had a few drinks just chillin. Jasmine told me she left him because he was abusive with her. He would talk down to her, and would embarrass her out in public. Then when they'd go out with his friends she had to watch what she said around his friends. He would get drunk then after work bring his friends over to their house. While she was sleeping he would pull the covers off of her and say to his friend's, look at that . . . How would you like sleeping with that every night?" I told Sandy.

Sandy slid the phone back over to me. She had never expected to hear anything like that. She didn't know what to think she was scared to death for me.

"Baby he said you were next what are you going to do?" Sandy asked.

"Put it in God's Hands then let Him fight my battles for me. The evil one will not gain victory here. God will show me what I need to do, and it'll be all right trust me it will be just fine" I replied.

"I think you should call that detective and let him know about that voice message. Baby, Listen to me I don't want anything bad to happen to you just let them do their job . . . LOOK AT ME JONATHAN! Don't get involved with that, you have too much to lose, think about us . . ." Sandy begged.

"Okay I'll call him now" I replied.

I picked up the phone called Detective Stone. Sandy got up ran to the bathroom trying to keep from crying. I'm learning that Sandy is very sensitive. Looks like she doesn't do very well under pressure. Having heard someone begging for their life while being murdered would be hard for anyone to deal with.

"Hello, Detective Stone this is Jonathan Paul speaking. I have a voice message on my phone I think you need to hear it. The murder of Jasmine Cooper was recorded on my cell phone; I can bring my phone to you tomorrow. What time do you get to the station? Okay, I'll see you at 7:00 am" I said.

I hung up the phone walked through the bedroom towards the bathroom to try to get Sandy to open the door.

"Sandy, may I come in?" I asked.

Sandy opened the door I walked into the bathroom and hugged her. She started crying like a baby we walked towards the bed then sat down. I tried to reassure her that everything was going to work itself out.

"Look Baby, it's going to be okay nothing is going to happen to me everything is going to be just fine. I told Detective Stone that I have the whole thing recorded on my phone. I'm going to take my phone to him tomorrow morning. He also he thinks he knows where this guy is staying. They'll stake out the building tomorrow morning, and try to pick him up. He won't even know what hit him. He also said he ran a trace on the license plate number I gave him, they're Texas plates" I said.

"Texas plates? What does that mean?" Sandy said.

"That's where the license plates are from." When Sandy left Texas to get away from her ex-boyfriend he followed her here to LA. He told Jasmine that if she were to leave him he would find her, and then kill her. Don't worry all of this will be over sooner that you think. When this is over, we can get on with our life okay?" I said.

"Jonathan, you're not going anywhere tonight, are you? Is it asking too much of you to stay here with me? We can turn on the fireplace downstairs. I can fix some crab legs, and then make us some more drinks. We can snuggle on the couch, watch some DVD's, can we do that?" Jasmine said.

"No, it's not asking too much baby. I have no plans on going anywhere tonight. I'll go downstairs light the fireplace, and find us some good movies to watch. After I take me a nice hot shower, I'll meet you in the living room on the couch JUST YOU AND I" I said.

Sandy reached for me we hugged then she went downstairs to start cooking up the crab legs. I went into the bathroom to take my shower, I could still hear Sandy crying I felt bad for her. I have to clean up this mess I made, starting tomorrow. I have a lot to be thankful for I thought to myself. Yesterday I landed a big contract with Supreme pictures, and now another project with Hollywood studios. It was time to turn up the flame a little higher. I have to call Bernard when I got out of the shower. I'm about to turn Hollywood upside down. Although I can't be in to places at the same time, but I can be two people in two different places at two different time's.

On one set I would portray myself as a white man. Then on Supreme set, I would be Jonathan. Bernard and Gerald will assist me in pulling off the biggest capper ever. I stepped out of the shower grabbed my towel dried off, and then walked over to a sunken dressing room and got dressed. As I started walking downstairs my phone began to ring. I sat on the couch took the remote control in my hand, turn on the TV, then put the phone to my ear.

"Hello . . ." I said.

It was Bernard he called to let me know that Jasmine's aunt came by earlier to talk to me about Jasmine.

"How you doing dog?" Bernard said.

"I'm good you know what? Man your goanna live a long time" I said.

"What? I hope so if you remember you almost got me killed back in college" Bernard said.

"You wanted to be a frat brotha Omega Phi Nu for life right?" I said.

"OMEGA Phi Nu! FOR LIFE . . . AHRU-RU!" Bernard said.

"Ok Look, I need to meet with you and Gerald tomorrow night" I said.

"I just started on this new show today. They say it's going to be a short day so I'm cool. I told my boss on the second job I won't be back, and that I quit" Bernard said.

"What did you do that for? What about your child support? How you going to deal with that?" I asked.

"I made an investment about two years ago with some stocks. My mother's boyfriend works for stock exchange. I dropped 20 grand on this deal, yesterday I made seven hundred thousand I owe forty thousand in child support. I'll send them their check tomorrow, and then I'll be straight with them" Bernard said.

"That's good Bernard you have to take care of your kids man. I'm happy for you Dog. So check this out I want you and your boy Gerald to meet me at Mulholland Point around 7:00 pm tomorrow night" Jonathan said.

"Hey I almost forgot . . . . That girl's aunt came by here looking for you tonight" Bernard said.

"What girl you talking about?" I said.

"The dead girl next door. What was her name?" Bernard said.

I became silent when Bernard started talking about Jasmine. It wasn't a very good subject for me to talk about. Sandy walked over to the couch with a tray of hot steamy crab legs, and a dish of melted butter. She sat the tray on the coffee table then returned to the kitchen for the drinks.

"Hey! I'll see the two of you tomorrow night. We'll talk . . . Right now I'm going to relax with my boo, I'll halla at you . . ." I said.

I hung up the cell phone, and set it on the coffee table. Sandy climbed onto my lap with the drinks in her hand. She handed me my drink then while holding my hand, she put the martini glass up to my mouth. Sandy reached into the silver platter grabbed a crab leg, dipped it into the hot melted butter, and then puts it into her mouth. She slid forward to feed me the other end of the crab leg. It was ever so sensuous. Sandy then slid beside me as she snuggled into my arms.

"Baby, who were you talking to?" Sandy said.

"Barnard, remember we were talking about him up stairs? Well, I guess I talked him up" I said.

"Baby, what are you watching?" Sandy said.

"What are you up to? What's with all the questions and what's up with all that 'Baby' stuff?" I said.

"Nothing, I'm just nosey like that. What's wrong? You don't you want me to call you 'Baby' like that?" Sandy said.

"Girl, I love everything you do it just reminds me of the times when my aunt would call me 'Baby'. It meant that she wanted something. I think you and I are starting to know one another very well. When you say Baby that way it gives me butterflies in my stomach" I said.

"You know what that means?" Sandy said.

"No, I don't what does it mean?" I asked.

"It means you're in love" Sandy said.

Sandy leaned forward straddled my lap took a piece of crab from the platter dipped it in the butter, and placed it in my mouth. She took another piece of buttered crab let it drip all over my chest. She then licked the warm butter from my chest all the while smiling as she looked deep into my eyes.

"You make me so happy I love you Jonathan. I can't wait to be Mrs. Jonathan Paul" Sandy said.

I touched Sandy's face then gently stroked her throat, as my fingers floated on her exotic soft caramel skin. I became lost in the windows of her soul. I felt the gravity as it pulled me towards her body. I kissed her on the forehead as her eyes fluttered shut. I placed another kiss behind her left ear near her collarbone she inhaled long, and deep. I felt her body vibrate as she moaned with pleasure then I kissed her soft wet lips.

The house phone rang. As I reached to answer it Sandy pushed my hand away, she wants all my attention.

"Baby, that's the house phone it could be your mother" I said.

I glanced at the ID caller.

"Yep. It's your mother . . . Hello Connie, What? Sandy's here with me . . . We're on our way" I said.

"What was that all about?" Sandy said.

"It's about your brother. Come on let's get dressed she wants us to meet her and your father at St. Gabriel's hospital. Your brother was arguing with a guy at a Gay club called The Audition. They got into it in the parking lot then the next thing you know Justin was shot" I told Sandy.

"Is he alright?" she asked.

"I don't know . . . Sandy is your brother Gay?" I said.

"Yes he is, mother wasn't sure but my dad knew Justin was different. He wasn't like the other little boys that lived in the neighborhood they played football, and he played with dolls" Sandy said.

"No matter what people my think about him, he is still family and he need us that's all that matters" I said.

We both rushed got dressed then we were out of the house and in the Porsche, flying down the street in no time. I was mashing' down Coldwater Canyon Road when I reached Sunset the car drifted to the left as I turn right on to Sunset Boulevard heading westbound. I was weaving in and out of traffic. Up ahead the light turned red at La Cienega I saw an opening in the traffic downshifted to second gear, and drifted right turning left onto La Cienega heading south.

I slapped the stick into first while mashin' out in second crossing Santa Monica Boulevard. I reached Beverly Boulevard down shifted to second, drifted left while turning right. The car fish-tailed and before we knew it, we were parked in front of St. Gabriel's Hospital. Sandy and I entered the hospital headed for the front desk inquired about her brother. The guard looked at her checklist.

"Justin Estrada? He's still in the emergency. Go down the hall to your right through the double doors. The nurse their can tell you where he is" the guard said.

We headed down the hallway through the double doors. Sandy stopped a nurse to ask about her brother, when her mother called out to us.

"I'm glad you two got here" Connie said.

"Is he going to be all right? Sandy asked.

"We don't know Sandy. The doctor told us to wait here, he'll be telling us something soon" Peter said.

"Who shot him?" Sandy asked

"The paramedics said the manager of the club heard Justin arguing about some comic book deal with this guy. Justin took a swing at him and knocked him to the ground. Then out of nowhere the guy pulled out a gun, and shot him twice in the chest" Connie said.

Just then detective Stone walked up with his partner Erika Winston. She was a white woman with blonde shoulder length hair. She stood about 5'9 weighed around 125 pounds. She had a tomboyish demeanor about her. She wore a grey sports jacket with a blue blouse some black jeans, and black hush puppies. As Erika stood next to Stone she puts her hand in her pockets. I could see her shield and gun sitting on her hip.

"Hello Mr. & Mrs. Zantex. Jonathan I just left the club about ten minutes ago. I spoke with one of the bouncers, and he said Justin was upset over a deal that went bad with his partner. Mr. Zantex is your son gay?" Detective Stone inquired.

"And if he is? What does that have do with him laying up in the emergency room with two holes in his chest?" Connie said.

"Ma'am, take it easy we don't mean to upset you" Erika said.

"Bitch, don't tell me to take it easy! That's my son in there fighting for his life. And you want to know if he's gay? You can kiss my . . ." Connie said.

"Mamma, Mamma! The doctor is here" Sandy said.

Doctor Shawn Matthews was a tall dark slender man with a beautiful smile. He was about six feet weighed around hundred and eight pounds. Dr. Matthews approached us then asked Connie, and Peter if they were Justin's parents.

"Yes I'm his mother and this is his father . . ." Connie said.

"Well, he's going to be fine you can see him for a moment. He's a little sedated so be short with your stay, he lost a lot of blood but he's going to be okay." Doctor Matthews said.

"Can I get those bullets from you? I need them for evidence" inquired Detective Stone.

"Sorry, no bullets they both were through and through. He was very lucky, the bullets entered very close to his heart. If they would have entered his body just a little lower he would have been toast, but he'll be fine he just needs lots of rest" Doctor Matthews said.

"Thank you Doctor" Connie said.

The doctor walked into the room to check Justin's vitals. Connie, Peter, Sandy and I followed the doctor into the room. Justin was lying in a bed with tubes connected to his body. His eyes were closed Peter, and Sandy stood by the side of his bed while Sandy held his hand. Detective Stone wanted to talk to Connie and I, so He took us out into the hallway to talk with us.

"I'm sorry if I sounded a little inconsiderate earlier. Here's the information I received from the bouncer. The guy that Justin hit was the shooter's lover. The disagreement was over a comic book deal that went bad. I also discovered that the guy Justin hit had just broken up with the shooter. Justin is the other victim's new lover. That's what I'm hearing. And yes this all is a little confusing to me too but check this out, the shooter drove off in a grey 09—300. The license plates read 1X-LOVER Now how you like them apples?" Detective Stone said.

"What are you saying?" Connie asked.

"I'm not sure, but I think the car that left the club is the same car that left the murder scene of Jasmine Cooper. Can you excuse us for a moment, I need to talk to Jonathan in private" Detective Stone said.

"We'll be in the room with the rest of the family detective Stone" said Detective Winston.

Detective Stone pulled me to the side as Connie left with Detective Winston. They all walked back into the room as I spoke with Detective Stone.

"You have something you want me hear?" he asked.

I grabbed my cell phone and retrieved the voice message for Detective Stone to hear.

"I just killed this two timing the snitch. I told her I would find her, and when I would, she was going to be a dead Bitch. It's your entire fault.

Don't nobody try and play me for a fool. Jonathan. That is your name, right? You're next. I'm coming for your ass. Just watch your back. That's all I can tell you . . ." said the voice on the phone.

"This guy is sick yeah we really need to get this son-of—a-bitch off the streets now! This was premeditated I know I'm going to need your phone as evidence. Come by my office later on today, you can pick it up then." Detective Stone said.

Detective Winston called Stone into the room. It looked as though Justin was waking up. Maybe what the detective was looking for was right in the next room. Detective, Stone and I entered the room. Stone walked over to the side of Justin's bed. As Justin looked up at the detective in a low tone with no anxiety in his voice I could hear the detective.

"How are you doing young man? I'm Detective Stone, and this here is my partner Detective Winston. You feel like talking son?" Stone said.

# THE CALL BACK

I was cruising down Melrose Boulevard and approached the front gate of Supreme Studios. I pulled up to the guard shack and flashed the black credit card that I was given at the party. The guard raised the gate, and I drove on to the lot then parked. I locked my car, and then headed over to Stage 9. As I walked onto the set I noticed that everyone was busy doing something. The FX people were rigging something up for a special smoke effect. I saw some extras walking around, they were made up to look like vampires, I thought that it was cool. The set looked like something out of a Frankenstein movie. It had gravestones planted in the ground a black backdrop around the entire set with blue lights overshadowing freshly dug graves. I exited the side door of the stage then walked over to where two trailers were parked side by side. At that point all I had to do was to just follow my nose.

"Hey look what the wind just blew in, my man! Jonathan! Omega Phi Nu until we die . . . AHRU, RU" Bernard said

"FO life my ninja . . . AHRU, RU. We need to talk. I know, I said we were supposed to meet tonight I was in the area so I stopped by, Look I need you to hook me up" I said.

"Okay, talk to me . . . what do you need me to do for you big brotha Jonathan?" Bernard said.

"Gerald, I'm going to need your help too. I want to pull off something that no one has ever done in Hollywood before. I'm under contract with Supreme; I cannot work for any other studios as Jonathan Paul right?" I said.

"You're right, so what are you trying to do man?" Bernard asked.

"I've been planning this for a while now and it's time to get it crackin'. Check it out . . . About two week's before I signed with Supreme I went on an audition. I didn't hear from them until yesterday. Now they want me to come back and read for them today . . . I want to do something crazy man" I said.

"Okay . . . what is it you want us to do for you? Let's hope that what you want is within reason. I would hate to be on Hollywood's Blacklist if you know what I mean, I want to keep my house on the hill, and my job. You feel me?" Gerald said.

"Don't worry, No one will ever find out about you or Bernard. They won't even know what hit them. It's a smooth idea Check it out. I want you to turn me into a Caucasian. I will go on this call back today as a white boy I'll lock it down, and then work on Supreme project as a Brotha, you feel me?" Jonathan said.

"Dude, what are you talking about? You'll be too tired to pull it off. You know how this game is played. You have to get your rest man you can't burn the candle on both ends like that. If you remember about two years ago this grip did four nights of golden time. Dog, it was the last day of shooting he left the set fell asleep at the wheel, and died bro. You can't do it . . . Jonathan" Bernard said.

"I have everything under control don't trip; I have all those details covered. Trust me it's a done deal all I need to know is if you guys will help me? We'll be rich and famous when it's all over. That new latex you have Gerald you did say it looks, and feels like real skin?" I said.

"That's right, and it won't take long to do either. We're looking at two hours tops to do your transformation. I'm down if your down with it Bernard" Gerald said.

"I'm with it . . . Let's do the damn thing" Bernard said.

Gerald took out a big plastic bowl from a cabinet on the wall. He poured some white powder in it along with a cup of liquid solution. He mixed it together until it became like a paste. Bernard took a straw, cut it in half, and then put both ends up my nose. As I lay back in a chair as Gerald put the paste all over my face. Gerald raised me up and had me lean forward to apply the paste on my head and neck, my entire head, and face was covered with paste that had to set for about thirty seconds.

Bernard pulled this wire from the side of my neck up and over to the other side of my head. I leaned forward as he held the mold as it slid on to his hands. Gerald worked on the back of my head until that piece came off. They set both pieces on a worktable then really went to work. Gerald poured latex into the face mold, and poured latex in the other half of the mold.

Bernard took a blow dryer and pointed it at the face mold as he dried the latex. The other half was done the same way. When it was ready

Gerald pulled the latex from the mold, and placed it on my face. He took a Sharpie marked areas to make a prefect placement on my face. Bernard started cutting the latex in pieces, and laid them out on a tray by a chair next to me. He began to put glue on the pieces of latex, and then arranged them on my face.

Thirty minutes had passed and it was finished. The transformation was done. I turned the chair around looked in the mirror at myself. Wow! I look like a combination of Brad Pitt and Val Kilmer. Bernard used a skullcap with jet-black human hair like those Elves Presley hairstyles. You couldn't even tell it was a hairpiece you could pull it, swim in it, and it wouldn't come off.

"What do you think"? Bernard said.

"What do I think? Ya'll hooked a brotha up! Who am I?" I said.

"You want to know who, I think you look like?" Gerald asked.

"Who am I?" I said.

"You look like Brad Pitt and Val Kilmer all in one dog, with that hair style dude you look like you just stepped out of a Vogue Magazine you know one of those top model gigs deals" Bernard said.

"That's what I'm talking about how does this sound? Shane Hilton, hum . . . A name like that sounds like you come from a very wealthy family . . . Shane Hilton" I said.

"Now alright . . . O my God, Shane Hilton you're a genius. No one will even have a clue as to who you are. I know who you are but . . . you are Shane Hilton I mean . . . Never mind you got it going on Jonathan. We're GOOD this is the best work I've seen us both do together yet!" Gerald said.

"Let me get the camera and take some shots . . . You look like a real white dude man! Gerald, this latex you hooked up is off the chain. You just took the makeup game to another level dog. This is what's going to make you rich, human like latex skin! In short we'll call it HLLS. We'll deal with that later. This right here . . . this shit is crazy" Bernard said.

"Okay guys look, I'm good with this I'm going to need some head shot can you hook me up?" I said.

"Yeah, I can do that follow me over to stage 11. Tamara used it this morning it's still hot. We can use their backdrop to shoot your pictures come on let's do this" Bernard said.

"I'll stay here just in case someone needs a touch up on the set. I'll hold down the fort while you do your magic I got this Bernard" Gerald said.

Bernard and I walked over to stage 11. As we got closer to the set, I noticed there were two sets. One was this beautiful landscape of the desert, and the other was a high-rise building. I went for the high-rise building it gave the illusion of being on top of the world.

In the corner of the set was a big industrial fan. We used it to make it look like the wind was blowing on top of the building. Bernard set up the lighting I stood on top of a make shift roof with a grey wall behind me. Bernard shined a light on me and against the wall. He began snapping pictures as the wind from the fan danced on my face.

Bernard had finished and we agreed that he would take more pictures at another day, but this was great. We went back to his office he took the chip from his camera then put it into his computer. He made thirty copies of each picture he took. Bernard made up a fake resume to go with the pictures, using his brother's name as my agent David Jenkins lll. Bernard also used his phone number as a contact in case someone would call he'd have my back. He knew exactly what to say.

My company was coming together I was going to knock the socks off these producer here in Hollywood. Every production company would come knocking on our door to use Gerald's HLLS for their shows. I would invest in Gerald's project then we would all make a killin.

Bernard showed me the finished product. The pictures it looked like I went to a professional studio and had them done. The resume was off the hook he made me look like an A-list actor from London. He also made a driver's license for me that looked very impressive. We shook hands, and then I was on my way to make history unfold. I hopped in my car crank up the Porsche and was rollin'. I got to Vine and Santa Monica hung a left then headed westbound. Just ahead was West Hollywood Studios I got into the left turning lane then drove onto the lot. I stopped at the guard shack gave him my name as Shane Hilton I was shocked! Dude raised the gate. I drove through now I had to make it past the casting director. I found a parking spot and whom do I see? It was Marty from the show I was working on early on this week, let's see how well Gerald and Bernard's magic worked. I got out of my car and made sure he saw me.

"Excuse me sir, can you help me? I have a call back for this show on this lot but since they started the new construction, I can't remember what side of the lot they were on. Would you know where the Robert Lang production company is?" I said.

"That's where I'm going since I'm going that way I'll walk with you" Marty said.

I reached into my pocket took out a pack of cigarettes. I opened the pack took out a cigarette and then put it in my mouth. I reached back into my pocket for my lighter but I couldn't seem to find it. I was making sure Marty was looking at me while I went through my trip.

"Man I'm nervous as hell . . . Damn I can't find any fire. You have a light?" I said.

"Sure, here you go. Who are you reading for?" Marty said.

"Marion Halls" I replied.

"Oh, she's good people she and I have worked on a lot of high action projects together" Marty said.

I lit his cigarette as we continued walking. A man and a woman in the parking lot were arguing by a parked car. She hauled off and slapped the shit out of him right in the face. He slapped her right back, she screamed while falling to the ground. I handed Marty my pictures, and then ran over to stop him from hitting her again.

"Dude . . . Dude! You can't hit a woman like that what's wrong with you?" I said.

"Oh, so you came to save her from getting her ass beat. Did you see what she did to me?" the bully said.

"It don't matter what she did to you. you're stronger than she is. And yeah, I saw her hit you and you're still standing right? Look what happened to her when you hit her, I bet you wouldn't hit a man like that!" I said.

The dude made a move like he was going to hit me that was the wrong thing to do. I turned my body to face dude he swung at me I took my right hand, and used it to deflect his left punch. With my left hand I deflected his punch, and then I shot a quick right backhand fist to his face sending him flying backwards. He started holding his face. With lighting speed I did a reverse spin-kick slapping him square in the face with the bottom of my shoe. The dude backed up again this time grabbing his nose Blood was all over his face. As he rushed forward in my on guard position I lunged forward with my right leg pushing off with my left leg planted firmly on the ground and kicked dude square in the chest. On impact lifting him up off the ground sending him flying backwards landing on the hood of a parked car.

He didn't even get up the strong impact of him hitting the car knocked him out cold. I ran over to where the woman was to see if she was okay. Marty was speechless he had never seen anything like that before. I think I scared him right away Marty started seeing dollar signs.

"Are you alright lady?" I said.

"I'm okay I think thank you for helping me, is there anything I can do for you?" Ramona asked.

The woman was in her late fifties, she had long beautiful steel grey hair just past her shoulder. She had it pulled back into a ponytail. She was a Caucasian with beautiful facial features and a great looking tan. She was a very nice looking woman with perfect measurements of 38-29-38. Ramona was wearing a red trimmed white tank top that showed off her rock hard abs. She wore skin-tight blue jeans, and sported a pair of hot red Stilettos she was as hot as a firecracker. Ramona liked to control her man with buying him things to keep him happy or to just to keep him around.

"I'm alright I was just concerned about you. He shouldn't have hit you like that" I said.

"I'm sorry let me introduce myself. My name is Ramona Reed I'm the executive Producer for Robert Lang Productions" she replied.

"Is that right? I was on my way to your office. I had a call back today, and I'm suppose to see Christina" I said.

"What part were you reading for?" Ramona asked.

"Detective Renzo, Ma'am" I replied.

"The next time anyone calls me Ma'am I am going to scream. Look, we will find someone for that part; I want you to be my leading man Markus Crenshaw. You are him I like the way you just took charge and just like that it was all over. Marty? I didn't see you during this entire commotion; it's a wonder I still know who I am, what is your name sweetheart?" Ramona asked.

"Shane Hilton . . ." I replied.

"You can call me Ramona. Enough with the Ma'am crap already. Marty, take him to Christina and tell her he's playing the part of Markus and get him a script please, you can take it from there. This is a sixteen-day shoot think about our budget and fit him in. I want to have enough left over to start on the next project alright? Thank you once again Shane" Ramona said.

"Ramona am I reading for the same person?" I asked.

"Shane, you will never have to read for anyone in this business you want to know why? You have a good spirit; well, he'll be moving out of my place today. You're a smart kid just keep in touch with Marty, and he will work everything out for you" Ramona said.

Ramona turned and walked towards her car as she continued talking to herself.

"I need to calm my nerves go to Macy's buy something for me for a change. I should have kicked his ass out long time ago but Lord I couldn't, He had some good old Mr. Good bar . . . Oh lord please forgive me because, I love me some young stuff" Ramona said as she walked off.

Ramona got in her car started it up put it into reverse then drove off. Out of nowhere her ex—boyfriend stepped out in front of her car. Ramona didn't stop she hit the gas pointed the car in his direction tapped him a little with the left front end of the car. That love tap sent him flying into another parked car. Sometime people just don't get it; they don't appreciate the things they have in life or the people in their lives. The only way they can communicate or show love is by being abusive. They underestimate everyone that crosses their path you have to be strong you have to stand up, and let you yes be yes, and your no be no.

I'm a soldier for life when I'm sent on a mission it's on and crackin. I always have to remind myself that we are our brother's keeper. Sometimes we can't control the things that happen to innocent people we just have to make good of a bad situations. Other times we can only do what is with in our power. There is a saying, "some people just don't believe that fat meat is greasy". You cannot do any wrong to God's children and think your going to get away with it. That's just not going happening because every dog will have their day, you can trust me on that.

Marty and I watched Ramona drive off of the lot. We turned around then headed towards the production office. Marty found Christina in her office he told her about the changes that were being made with my character. He told her to draw up a contract for Shane Hilton.

"Ramona didn't tell me what we should pay you for this project. Let's see . . . She gave you the leading role and from the work you've done and from what I can see, hum sixteen day shoot . . . Hold on, let me call Ramona . . ." Marty said.

Marty whipped out his cell phone then dialed Ramona's number. Christina walked over to a file cabinet opened it reached inside, and pulled out a script. She closed the cabinet walked back to where I was then handed me a script that read, "Revenge" on the front cover.

"Ramona darling, I'm trying to come up with some numbers for Mr. Hilton. This is just a sixteen-day shoot right? That's in the budget ok, no backend residuals got it . . . Okay sweetheart talk to you later smooches," That woman will talk you to death, but I love her" Marty said.

Damn, I couldn't call Bernard to give him a heads up on what's going on. Marty had my resume in his hand then took a seat at Christina's desk. He pulled up a program on the computer and clicked on "Contracts" He looked at my picture with a strange look on his face.

"Who took these pictures?" Marty asked.

"A friend of mind who does a little freelancing on the side" I said.

"Tell him he has a very good eye, well first things first. Let me call your agent and let him know what we've decided to do . . ." Marty said.

I was beginning to have a problem with the latex on my face. Under my chin it was starting to itch. I was afraid that it would rip, if I scratched it, I had to think fast.

"Excuse me, where is your men's room?" I asked.

"Go to the end of the hall and make a right" Christina said.

Briskly I made my way down the hall. I found the restroom once inside I walked over to the mirror and looked at my face. I held my chin up to see if anything was peeling off. I pulled the latex on my chin, but nothing happened. I began to scratch the area that itched under my chin a little harder.

"Damn, this here is some strong stuff," I thought to myself I had this latex on for about two hours now and it still looked fresh. There was no sagging, wrinkling or peeling. This is way cool I thought I'd pay a visit to the Club tonight and see if Mr. 1X-LOVER came out to play.

The latex fit snugly on my face like a glove. I moved my head to the left worked my mouth from side to side, then tightened my jaw to see if the latex could pass the test. I flushed the toilet washed my hands, and ran my fingers through my hair. I combed it backwards then placed a wave in the front, as I let a curl hang down over my right eye.

I left the restroom then joined Marty and Christina back in the production office. Marty was finished with my contract he prints out a copy and handed it to me. I looked it over and liked the numbers they came up with.

"I want let my people look at these figures if they feel the same way about them as I do, we can move forward. I'll call you in a few days is that alright?" I said.

"Today is Wednesday I should hear from you around Friday. Shooting starts next Tuesday so learn your lines. We'll see you on Friday. While you were in the restroom I talked to your agent David he seems to be a pretty cool fella, well welcome aboard" Marty said.

Marty and I shook hands and for a split second I felt as though he recognized me. He couldn't quite place where he had seen me before, but It would come to him soon enough.

"You know, I always told David that he missed his calling he's a real funny guy, we'll talk soon" I said.

I left the production office got in my car started it up put it in reverse and drove off. I had to pick up my phone from Detective Stone and that might not be so easy, he's a pretty sharp guy well, let's see if my plan will work as Jonathan's assistant.

I pulled up in front of the police station and parked. I got out of my car closed the door walked into the police station. Tonight was a very busy night at the police station there was a woman standing at the watch commander's desk giving him the blues about a stolen car.

"Ma'am, I can't help you if you don't calm down" the watch commander said to her.

"My husband bought that car for me as a birthday present. I haven't had that car twenty-four hours and somebody has stolen it. I'm trying to tell you what happened but you won't listen to me" the woman said.

"Okay, I listened to you now you listen to me. Fill—out this report and when you're done I can help you! I cannot help you if you don't fill out a report, do you understand? Sir Can I help you?" the watch commander said to me.

"I'm looking for Detective Stone" I said.

"He works over in Homicide. Go through that glass door make a right you'll see him" the watch commander said.

"This door right here? Thanks" I said.

I walked through the glass door and stood by a cubical looking for Stone. From a distance I could see Detectives Stone, and Winston talking to one other. I walked over to where Stone and Winston were sitting.

"Hello, I'm looking for Detective Stone" I said.

"I'm Stone and are you?" said Detective Stone.

"My name is Shane Hilton I'm Jonathan Paul's personal assistant. He told me to come get his phone, He would have done it himself but he is on the set filming. Today was their first day of shooting, and things can get very busy so he ask me to get his phone for him" I told him.

I was so convincing that Stone didn't even ask to see my ID. Stone reached into his desk grabbed the cell phone and gave it to me.

"To be on the safe side can you show us some ID just in case the phone doesn't get to him? I'm sure you understand" Detective Winston said.

I look at Detective Winston then at Detective Stone. Slowly I reached into my back pocket took out my wallet then showed her my ID. It read "DMV London driver License Expires 10-16-16 Shane Hilton 124 Pillion Street, Liverpool, Sex: M HGt: 6'-00 Hair: Blk Wt: 180 Eye: Hazel, DOB: 10-16-86"

"You're good, just doing our job Mr. Hilton. By the way are you related to the famous Hiltons?" Detective Winston asked.

"As a matter of fact yes I am I'm the Nephew. I understand you have all types of games played on you. I see your job is not an easy one. Well, I need to get back and get this phone to Jonathan, you've been a big help" I said.

I left the police station then called Bernard to give him the good news about the call back. I truly loved Sandy I would never do anything to hurt her. But there was something I had to do to make things right for myself. A monster murdered an innocent woman, he was someone that Jasmine was very afraid of, and I know the feeling. This person controlled her mind in a twisted demented way; it reminded me of how my father was to me. I understood how she felt, I had to go under deep, deep cover to play a role true to life in order to catch Jasmine's killer. The way he murdered her was no justification for it. I'm going to use myself as bait to get next to Jasmine's killer. I would gain his confidence then turn the tables on him.

"Bernard were in, I met the executive producer of the show in a strange way today. A guy was beating the crap out of her, and I stopped him" I said.

"What do you mean you stopped him? You didn't kick his ass did you?" Bernard said.

"Well, something like that anyway she told me she was the executive producer, and that she wanted to thank me for helping her. She bumped me up to the leading role for helping her out in the parking lot, they want to give me $10,000.000 to play the lead.

"What did you say? Marty called me we talked but he never said anything regarding that kind of money. $10,000.000? What kind of show is it?" Bernard asked.

I'm not sure I think it's a pilot for a new TBO show. If it works out it's on and cracking, I think it's like CSI or the Wire" I said.

Jonathan, do you hear yourself? You're pushing the envelope to far dog! I told you're ass already man you can't pull it off. You won't have the energy to do both shows. It sounds like you have a death wish, But it's your life right? You might think you can work on that show during the day and the other at night, I don't know man you need to really think that one over," Bernard said.

"Are you with me? It's going to work don't worry. I just need you and Gerald to have my back" I said.

"I got you dog . . . you're like a brother to me man. I would hate to see anything bad happen to you behind your crazy antics" Bernard said.

"They want me to get back to them by Friday. I told them I wanted my people to look at the contract before I gave them an answer" I said.

"That was smart okay, take it over to them on Friday I'm sure they will fill you in on the other details" Bernard said.

"Okay look I'll call you later I need to check out something. I'll come by your place later to let you see the contract, and then you can take this shit off my face alright I'll talk to later" I said.

I hung up the phone and noticed that the sun was going down. The reflection of skyscrapers shone through the window of my car. As I zoomed down the freeway passing other cars it was like being trapped in a Matrix. Over to my right was Chocolate City a place where nobody sleeps. A place where people plot against one another for sex and drug's, a city where the crack monsters live and disorder would rule the night. From the freeway you could see inside the office buildings. Some had lights on and others were pitch black cold and empty looking. The brown ghost like structure's protruding from the ground had lots of stories to tell. If only I could be that fly on the wall to see what happens to the people in that world and why did it stopped for them. You have to keep it pushing until you reach your destination. Never give up on your dreams; if you do your life will never be the same you'll end up in a cardboard penthouse on some side street eating rats and sharing you space with roaches while tweaking your life away. I couldn't tell Sandy what I was about to do I hated that I had to keep this a secret. It was the only way to bring this guy to justice. That's the way I saw it, and that was the way it was going to go down.

I called Sandy to check in with her. I didn't want her to start worrying about me. I had to do some quick thinking because I was going to the club to set a trap for Jasmines killer. I had to keep everything under wraps or she'd bust me, I couldn't slip up.

"Hey Babe! How are you doing? Where are you? Look, I'm going to pick up a few things from Bernard's. He's going to help me choose the guys for the wedding party. We have one week left, and after that you'll be Mrs. Jonathan Paul," I said.

"I can't wait to be your wife Jonathan it will be the happiest moment of my life" Sandy said.

"Everything is working out I feel the same way you do just a little nervous. I know that this feeling will soon pass, how's your brother doing?" I said.

"He's out of ICU he's okay he cussed out the nurse tonight over something about his food being too cold. He's alright though trust me" Sandy said.

"I'll see you when I get home, love you babe" I said.

"I love you more don't be out too late or you're going to have me worrying about you" Sandy said.

"I'll be fine, I'll call you when I'm leaving is that cool baby?" I said.

"Yeah it's cool baby just be safe," Sandy said.

"Always" I said.

Man, I hated to do that. I hung up the phone and then laid it down on the passenger seat, then made my way to the club. I down shifted to second popped the clutch as the he G-force pushed me back into the seat as my Porsche screamed down Highway 101.

# THE AUDITION

I look into my rear view mirror to see if everything on my face was still intact. I looked out of my front windshield onto the parking lot, and saw two men standing talking to one another. They looked like they were enjoying their conversation. I gave myself a moment to gather my composure before I transformed into my dark side. I got out of my car, locked the door, and reached into my back pocket to take out a pack of cigarettes. As I lit up I glanced at the marquee on the building it read, "The Audition". I took a long puff, and then slowly began walking towards the club. I knew that I would fit in with my black leather pants, wide black silver studded belt, black leather boots. And my white wife beater that showed off a tattoo of a swimming dragon breathing out smoke from his nostrils. I thought that my diamond—studded earring was working and my hair looked cool with a curl hanging over my right eye. I knew I would raise some eyebrows. I headed for the front door of the club once Inside I stood by the bar then ordered a green apple martini. I positioned myself against the counter then turned my body to face the pool table. A game had just ended so I walked over to the pool table to join the winner.

"Looks like you need a player" I said.

"You wanna play?" the winner said.

"I'd like to, are you here with someone? Or are you just cruising?" I said.

"I cruise where ever go it keeps the peace, and I don't like string attachments" the winner said.

I walked over to the back wall where the pool stick rack was. I took a pool stick from the rack, and walked back to the table. The waitress brought my drink to the pool table, and I dropped a twenty on her tray.

"Ah, hold on sweet heart" I said.

I turn my attention to the pool player and I noticed he wasn't drinking anything. He was a white male he wore black jeans black boots and a shirt opened in the front. Kind of grunge-like about 5'-11" 175 pounds with short salt, and pepper hair, his name was Chris Dalton.

"What's your name man?" I said.

"Chris Dalton, You can call me Dalton that's what everybody calls me around here" he said.

"What's your poison Dalton?" I asked.

"What do your friends call you?" he asked.

"Shane, Shane Hilton" I replied.

"It's nice to meet you Shane, My Poison? Sex on the Beach . . . Any relation to the famous Paris Hiltons?" Dalton asked.

"Bring him a Sex on the Beach, and keep the change" I said.

The waitress took the money put it in her pocket then walked off.

"I'm her nephew, my family and I just moved back to the states to help out with the family business. My aunt is building another Hotel in West Hollywood near Century City, she wants my dad to manage it for her" I said.

"That's cool . . . where are you from?" Dalton said.

"London England, I lived in the same town where the Beatles are from" I said.

Dalton racked up the balls on the table.

"Go ahead Shane you can bust first" Dalton said.

Dalton likes to talk he knows everybody that comes through those Audition doors. If there is something you want to know about someone in the club Dalton, has the low down on them.

"What do you do for a living Dalton?" I said.

"I work in the entertainment business. I work in the wardrobe department at Samsung Rich studios on Santa Monica Boulevard. I've been there now going on seven years. That was the first job I ever had since out of high School . . . What do you do Shane?" Dalton said.

"I'm an actor" I said.

"I know you have heard this before—everybody in Los Angeles is an actor or a rapper. Good for you, do you live around here?" Dalton said.

"I live in Studio City" I replied.

"You know, everyone that comes in here works in the entertainment business even down to the bar tender. He's a stand-in for Christen Blather during the day, and he grinds here till closing. I come here every day after work, play a little pool or get my freak on in the men's room. If I'm lucky

I might leave here with some company you know what I mean" Dalton said.

The waitress came back with Dalton's drink she set trey on the edge of pool table next to Dalton.

"What do we toast to?" Dalton said.

"Let's toast to a long life in the world of entertainment" I replied.

Just like clockwork Jasmine's killer walked into the club. He sat at the bar looked around the room as if he were looking for some one. Dalton and I continued to play our game. I glanced over and made eye contact with the killer I nodded my head, and he did the same. The killer turned to the bar ordered a green apple martini from the bar tender. I ask Dalton about the guy that just walked in.

"He looks a little dangerous. I'd like to get to know him. What do you know about the guy sitting at the bar?" I said.

"Oh that's DL, he just moved here from Texas . . . he's a little strange piece of fruit" Dalton Said.

"What do you mean? I said.

"Well, He comes in here from time to time. He'll play a little pool have a few drinks then leave. Early this week he and two other guys got into a big fight. Then they took it to the parking lot in the back, next thing you know one of the guys ended up shot. This is the first time I've seen him since that incident. I think the guy that got shot was named Justin. The manager said they took him down the street to St. Gabriel's hospital" Dalton said.

"His name is DL? What kind of name is that?" I said.

"I don't know how true this is but the word on the street is that he's a hit man. Like I said, I don't know true it is, so don't quote me on it. Remember . . . you didn't hear it from me, if you know what I mean" Dalton said.

"A hit man, Is that right? I would like to get to know him" I said.

"Hey Shane, I would play the rest of this game out but I have to leave. I need to take my dog out for his walk. Thanks for the drink and I'll see you around. Maybe we can do the Roxie one night then the next morning, we can do breakfast. Oh, you have something white next to your eye you want me to blow it off?" Dalton said to me.

"Thanks man I got it, you take care of yourself we'll talk again soon" I said.

Dalton hung his pool stick on the wall then left. As he walked out of the club DL watched him, like a pit bull ready to attack. He then looked over at me as I racked up the balls on the table. DL grabbed his drink left the bar, and walked over to the pool table where I was.

"Do you play?" I said.

"A little, do you play for money?" DL said.

"I like to gamble but when I play this game I like to play for fun. It relaxes me when I have, something on my mind" I said.

"Is that right? Is this your first time here?" DL said.

"Yeah, I was in the area I saw the marquis announcing the Audition so I thought I'd check it out" I said.

"Where you from?" DL said.

I felt a little insulted by the way he asked that question. I put the pool stick down walked towards DL and got in his face to set him straight. I wasn't going to let anyone talk to me in that way specifically him.

"What do you mean where am I from? Do I have to have your permission to be in here? I thought this was a free country, and a man could go wherever he likes. Where are YOU from?" I said.

"Hold up FRIEND . . . I didn't say that to upset you. I heard your accent and I couldn't place it, I wasn't trying mad dog you. Can I buy you a drink?" DL said.

DL motioned to the waitress to come to the pool table. She was with a customer when he got her attention. DL looks at my glass and noticed that he and I were drinking the same drink.

"How you doing? What can I get for you tonight Mr. DL? I know you want a green apple martini right?" the waitress said.

"Make those, two green apple martinis" DL Said.

"Two "green" apple martinis coming right up" the waitress said.

I took the pool stick aimed it at the center ball. I shot the white ball in the direction of the cluster of balls in the center of the table. I knocked the solid green ball in the left pocket and the solid yellow ball into the right corner pocket. They all fell in at the same time DL just looked at me with a half sneer look on his face.

"Not bad you look like you know what you're doing with that stick. Look, I think we got off on the wrong foot my bad. They call me DL" he said.

"Shane Hilton" I replied.

"Well, it's nice to meet you Shane Hilton no hard feelings?" DL said.

"I'm cool. What kind of work do you do DL?" I said.

"I'm in the extermination business you know getting rid of creepy things nasty bugs. The company I use to work for was based in Texas. After hurricane Katrina things were not the same anymore. Work got slow then the company bellied up. So I came to LA to get my hustle on, in the land of milk and honey what's your story? DL said.

"I'm from London I grew up in a small town called Liverpool. My family and I moved here about three weeks ago, I work in the entertainment business" I said.

"Everybody that comes through here works in the entertainment world what do you do in that world?" DL said.

"I'm an actor" I replied.

The waitress came back with our drinks she set them down on the edge of the pool table. DL gave her a fifty-dollar bill then told her to keep the change. I was really trying to keep my cool and stay in character, I wanted this guy dead real bad. I wanted to make him suffer for all the sins he has committed. I had a small vile of green anti-freeze in my pocket that matched the color of his martini. While DL was flirting with the waitress I walked up behind him and poured the anti-freeze in his glass. I took the glass nearest to me took a drink then walked back to the end of the pool table. Part of me didn't want to hurt this man but another part urged me to do it. Maybe it was because of the abuse I had experienced at the hand of my father. I had a flashed back off the fear I heard in Jasmine's voice on the day she was killed. I decided then to avenge her death, and make DL suffer a slow painful death.

I set my drink on a table near the back wall. Then took the pool stick and ran the resin cube over the tip of it. I looked at DL and saw him wearing a half smile on my face. The waitress walked away and DL looks down at his drink He reached for it, and took a sip then looked at me.

"This drink is to die for. I don't know if it's because it's my second drink of the night, but I'm feeling pretty good right about now. You look like you're ready to play, come on let's do this" DL said.

As I began to take my shot I could tell that the drink was starting to take an effect on him. He appeared very happy then suddenly he became depressed, and then broke out into a cold sweat. I decided to watch him finish his drink then leave.

"Hey check this out DL I have to make a run. Let's finish our drinks you can give me your number and I'll call you later on this week, maybe we can hook up, and do something together" I said.

DL tipped his glass and finished his drink. By that time he was seeing double. He didn't look well he was starting to sweat profusely. I walked over to where he was standing it looked like he needed to sit down.

"Hey man, you don't look so good I think you might be coming down with the flu. It's going around you know maybe you need to go to the doctor and get that checked out" I said.

I walked DL over to the bar he took a seat on a barstool. He asked the bartender for a pen and paper.

"Alright, I got your number now like I said I'll call you next week to see if we can, do this again all right? I said.

I left the club and was on my way to Bernard's to get this mask off then home. I had to disengage from the Shane character and return to myself. It just hit me I thought I had taken on something that I should have put a little more thought into. Having to take on two personalities could make you lose sight of reality. Trying live two lives won't work for me, but I had to do this for Jasmine. I got into my car closed the door, and gave myself a moment before calling Sandy.

This Saturday I was going to become a married man. Next month the project with Supreme studios would begin. It was going to be a challenge for me to do both projects but that's what gets me off. The more complex things become the better I adapt.

"How you doing baby? I'm on my way home do you want me to pick anything up for you before I get home?" I said.

"That's so sweet of you Baby. I'm not at home I'm with mother I'll be leaving shortly. We're going over some last minute things for the wedding Papa wants this to go over in a big way. Remember I am his only little girl, and daddy gives me whatever I want, and what I want is a big beautiful wedding!" Sandy said.

"Okay, I'm going to stop off at Baskin Robbins. I have a taste for some pistachio Ice cream, what do you want?' I said.

"Oooo I want some peach cobbler Ice cream with pralines. I don't know if they have it or not you might have to buy both baby well, ok see you at the house love you Baby!" Sandy said.

"Love you too sweetheart talk to you in minute. Tell mother hello for me. Can I tell you something?" I asked.

"You sure can" Sandy said.

"I want you to know that you make me very happy. After this Saturday, you'll be my wife. I'm going to love you until the day I die, you complete me" I said.

"My rib forever, you'll always be in my heart nothing, and no one will ever break us apart. I love you too . . . Mr. Jonathan Paul" Sandy said.

# LIKE AN ANGEL

This day was a very sad one for me Sandy and I had to catch a flight to Fort Worth Texas to bury a very dear friend of mine. Today was Jasmine's funeral it was held at First Wedgwood Baptist Church. It's a very beautiful church it seats about five hundred people. It is adorned with high vaulted ceilings soft lines in the white wooded rafters. You know when you are in the house of God, it has forty-foot unfinished white marble walls, and stained glass windows with holy scribes on them. Pew's on both sides of the church rest on a crimson red carpet that lead from the north exit foyer to the front of the church. Seated in the pews were Jasmine's friends and family. Beside the pulpit is a large life-like statue of Jesus Christ on the cross with His head in a downward position. Beneath the pulpit on the floor was a soft pink casket trimmed in white ivory inside the casket laid Jasmine Cooper.

Dressed in a beautiful white suite she looked like a sleeping angel. At the head and at the foot of the casket were yellow and white roses with lavender Baby's Breath. On top of the casket was a large arrangement of white roses that filled the church with the scent of sweet honeysuckle.

The gentle voices of the choir sang "Soon and Very Soon". In the front pew sat Jasmine's father, mother and teenage brother. Behind them sat her Aunt and other family members as they wept. Everyone was dressed in black. Jasmine's mother was wearing dark glasses to hide the tears she was shedding for her dead daughter.

The invocation & prayer was done by Rev. ST Williams Jr. The opening sentence for worship was read from Ecclesiastes 3:1-4; 11-12. Rev. Williams stands 5'7" and weighs around 180 pounds he resembles a football player in his late thirties neat and clean cut dressed. His head is shaven and he wears a long white robe with a red sash over his shoulder. He wore black Armani dress shoes and a large silver cross on his chest.

"Good afternoon family and friends of Jasmine Cooper. If you take your bibles from the pews you can read with me from Ecclesiastes 3:1-4. Let me know when you're there" Pastor Williams said.

"Amen . . ." the people responded.

"There is time for everything, and a season for every activity under heaven. A time to be born and a time to die a time to plant and a time to uproot, a time to kill, and a time to heal, a time to tear down and a time to build a time to weep and time to laugh a time to mourn and a time to dance. Now, turn with me to Ecclesiastes verse 11-12. When you're there, say "Amen" Pastor Williams said.

"Amen . . . the people replied.

"'He has made everything beautiful in its time he has also set eternity in the hearts of men; yet they cannot fathom what God has done from beginning to end. I know that there is nothing better for men than to be happy and do well while they live'. That ends the reading. Amen" Pastor Williams said.

"Amen . . ." the people replied.

"There is a time for everything, and a season for every purpose under heaven" Pastor Williams added.

"A time to be born, and a time to die" the people responded.

"A time to plant, and a time to uproot" Pastor Williams said.

"A time to kill, and a time to heal" the people said.

"A time to tear down and a time to build" said Pastor Williams.

"A time to weep, and a time to laugh" the people said.

"A time to mourn and a time to dance" said the pastor.

"He has made everything beautiful in its time" the people said in unison.

"He has also set eternity in the hearts of men, yet they cannot fathom what God has done from beginning to end" said the pastor.

"I know that there is nothing better for men than to be happy and do well while they live. Glory be to the Father, and to the Son, and to the Holy Spirit. As it was in the beginning is now and ever shall be" Said Pastor Williams.

"Amen" the people responded.

Jasmine's aunt sang "Take Me Back", which was followed by a reflection by a co-worker, and another by her nephew. After the choir sang "Be blessed" family members said their goodbyes. A slideshow featuring

Jasmine's life was presented. A pallbearer approached the casket, and opened it for a final viewing.

The ushers started directing people from the back to the front of the church to view the casket. Before exiting the church friends and family members hugged Jasmine's mother, and father as the choir sang "Going up yonder". Sandy and I viewed the casket, and then walked towards Jasmine's mother. I knelt down to hug her she whispered into her ear "Thank you for coming". She looked up at me, and wiped the tears from my eyes then cupped her hands around my face. She pulled me towards her face and kissed me on the cheek. I shook Jasmine's father's hand Sandy took Jasmine's mom's hands, and kissed her on the cheek. Sandy shook Jasmine's father's hand as we walked out of the church.

There was a long precession of cars lined up along the curb at Forest Lawn. After cars were parked everyone walked over to a white carriage with six white horses hitched to the front of it. After the driver boarded the carriage the driver cracked a whip, and the horses headed towards the mausoleum where Jasmine's body was laid to rested. Once at the mausoleum six men pulled the soft pink casket from the back of the carriage. Framed in etched glass were flying white doves. The casket was taken inside for a final word then Jasmine's body was sealed inside a white marble wall. A group of people gathered around a man who stood outside with a cage of white doves. Jasmine's family gathered around the man holding the doves who put a dove in Jasmine's nephew's hand. The nephew lightly tossed the dove in the air then the dove engaged in flight high in the sky.

Again, the man opened the cage reached inside, and pulls out two more white doves. This time he gave a dove to Jasmine's brother and niece. Once in the sky the doves caught up to one another circled overhead then flew west in a V formation. Only the close family members entered the mausoleum, along with some men all dressed in black suites wearing dark sunglasses. These men were DL's brothers. They wanted to pay their respects and to see if DL did what he was ordered to do.

Six months ago someone saw Jasmine talking to an undercover FBI agent posed as a Priest. He would listening to her talk about different hits that were about to go down. It troubled her to know what was about to happen, and if any of her business partners found out She feared losing her job because of the type of business her husband was in. There was a contract out on a High official; DL was the person that pulled the trigger, in the assassination of Mayor Rufus Brown. The mayor was in charge of a shipment of black heroin on the docks that came in at 2:00am. DL's brother's was there ready to make the pickup that night.

Mayor Rufus Brown crossed DL's boss they were met by DEA agents they never had a chance. Shots rang out between the DEA agents and DL's brothers. They were all shot execution style, the dope and 2.5 million dollars came up missing. In turn the FBI agent told DL's mob boss how he got the information. The boss would later have a meeting with DL, the boss told him that Jasmine had to be dealt with, and if he didn't do it, they would deal with her themselves, and he would be next.

Jasmine was upstairs in the bedroom about to make a call on the house phone. She picked up the receiver and overheard DL talking to his boss about what was expected of him. So she packed up her things that night sneaked out of the house, and caught the first thing smoking out of Texas. Jasmine knew her life was over so she came to LA to get away from DL, and to buy herself a little more time.

Rev. ST Williams was standing in front of the casket saying some last words of comfort to Jasmine's family then ended the service in prayer for the repast.

"Our Father, who art in heaven, hollowed be Thy Name. Thy kingdom come thy will be done on earth as it is in heaven. Give us this day our daily bread and forgive our trespassers as we forgive those who trespass against us. And lead us not into temptation but deliver us from evil. For Thine Is the kingdom, and the power, and the glory forever, and ever. Father, bless this food that we are about to partake. We ask you to bless the hands that are preparing this wonderful meal for this accusation in Jesus name we pray. Amen" Pastor Williams said.

Jasmine's father walked towards Sandy and I and gave us directions to the repast at their house. Sandy and I walked out of the mausoleum towards a black SUV Navigator. As we walked across the courtyard, I noticed a black limo parked facing in the same direction we were walking in. Little did we know in the backseat of that limo was DL. He was not looking so well he had a reddish-looking rash around his neck, and was sweating real bad. He was coughing up blood into a handkerchief. We walked past the limo as DL rolled up the window. His brother got into the limo from the street side. DL was too sick to recognize who I was slowly the limo pulled off.

"Well" DL said through his coughing. "How was the service?"

"It was real nice the reverend gave a good sending off speech for that rat" Joey said.

"How did she look?" asked DL though a cough. I kind of messed her up real bad but that's how the game is played you get caught slipping you get dealt with". Said D. L

"Man, she looked very nice. She was dressed in a white suit. She looked like an angel sleeping, DL man what's up with up you? You alright?" Joey said.

"I'm fine; I think I'm coming down with the flu man. Okay fellas, I'm flying back to LA on a red eye tonight. There's a party going on in the Hollywood Hills and I have to be there. It's about a new assignment. So now we all have to step up are game, you feel me?" DL said.

"Alright, we have this here taken care of do your thing and we'll be right here. If you need some backup just call me. DL, you need to really have yourself checked out you coughing up blood like that Dude, that's not good" Joey said.

"Joey, don't even go there I'm fine" I said! "We'll leave it at that. I'm not going let you put that on me. I'm good dog that's on everything I love. The only person who can take me out of this game is God Himself, not a man on this earth can stand up to me because I'm immortal" DL said.

Back at the repast Sandy and I sat on a couch talking to Jasmine's aunt who lives in LA. She was the last person to really know what was going on with Jasmine before she moved away from her home.

"She was a sweet little girl she always wanted to help people. When she turned sixteen I asked her what she wanted to be when she was finished with school. She told me she wanted to be a public defender. She always worked hard for the underdog in all of her cases. I used to ask her why she would go out of her way to help these people. She told me that the state didn't believe them, but she always did. With her straight forward approach she won every case" Jasmine's aunt said.

Jasmine's aunt had fair skin brown and gold streaks in her hair it rested on her shoulders in a blunt cut. She had green eyes and the bone structure in her face was like a woman in her thirties. She had a caramel bronze completion about 5'2" 95 pounds and she wore a black low cut backless tight fitting dress. It was high in the front near her thigh with a teardrop cascade in the back along with black stilettos, to complement the dress.

She wore a close fitted black hat with a black veil covering her face. She had a very sexy look and was a very classy lady.

"She told me you were very nice to her and that you were the first person she met when she moved to that building. She didn't make many friends in my neighborhood. She worked late nights and sometimes wouldn't get home until 4:00 a.m. Jasmine was a hard worker" said the aunt.

"One morning, I was getting ready for work and had my music up a little too loud. I think she had just gotten home from work that morning. She knocked on my door and asked me if I could turn my music down. It was keeping her up, and she couldn't sleep that's how we met" I told Jasmine's aunt.

"And who is the pretty lady sitting next to you?" asked Jasmine's aunt.

"This is my fiancé, Sandy Zantex were getting married this Saturday you are welcome to come. It's going to be at St. Paul Evangelical Lutheran Church in Los Angeles" I said.

"I know where that is 3901 West Adams Boulevard I know exactly where that is. It's the white church on the corner they call it the light house" said the aunt.

"That's it. The wedding will start at two o'clock and the reception will follow at the Beverley Hills Hilton soon after the wedding" Sandy said.

"Okay, I wouldn't miss it for anything in the world" said the aunt.

Just then, Jasmine's mother walked into the rooms she was wearing a long tight-fitting black dress with black high heels. She was an older version of Jasmine she was 5'7" 120 pounds. She wore diamonds on her hands around her neck, and she wore the hell out of a pageboy haircut, her name was Marine Cooper.

"Did I hear someone say they're getting married this weekend?" Marine said.

"Yes ma'am you did, this is Sandy Zantex, she's going to be my bride this Saturday you're welcome to come" I said.

"Why, that's nice of you! I'll come with my sister let me ask you something, do you know who took my baby away from me? The detectives told my sister and I that you were there what happened?" Marine said.

Not exactly, I saw her just before I left the building that morning. Mostly elderly people live in that building, we all look out for one another. I was on my way to my agent's office when I got a call from Jasmine. She said her ex-boyfriend was kicking her door in. I rushed over to help her, but I was too late. My brother called 911 and moments later CSI detectives came along with Hollywood PD they asked me some questions and that was it" I said.

"Did I hear you say her ex-boyfriend? That's DL! I never liked that man any way. He's mixed up with some very bad people. I told her to leave him alone a long time ago and that he was nothing but trouble for her" Marine said.

"One day, he was by my house she went out to the car with him. I kept hearing her tell him she didn't tell anybody anything. Before he left I heard him say that if he found out that she talked to the FBI he was going to kill her. She moved out the next day" said the aunt.

"The police have a few leads to his whereabouts they're on to him. They'll catch him it's only a matter of time. Trust me he's going to get what's coming to him and more" I said.

"I sure hope that they do catch him, and when they do I want him dead. I want him to get the death penalty! I'm sorry it was wrong for me to say that. Why did he take my baby away from me? She looked good didn't she? My baby looked like a sleeping angel" said Marine.

Marine started to cry as her sister hugged her to console her then helped her up and took her to her to a bedroom to lay her down to get some rest.

"You two make yourselves at home go and get yourselves something to eat I'm going to lay her down. She needs to rest this is too much for her I'll come and talk with you later, okay?" said the aunt.

"We'll be right here if you need us for anything" I said.

"I see why my Jasmine liked you so much you are so helpful. Sandy, you got yourself a good man. Don't let him get away from you he's a keeper" Marine said.

Yes sir . . . I have a few things up my sleeve to help apprehend this killer. No one deserves to die the way Jasmine did. No matter what she told the FBI he still should of had her back. If he loved her he could have worked something out, and got her a pass. But that's the business the game doesn't change just the players. You always have someone who wants to make their own rules, and wants to change things to suit themselves. But there's an old saying, sometimes the hunter can fall in to his own trap, and soon become the prey.

# FLU SYMPTOMS

DL was on his way to Dallas Fort Worth Airport. The limo he was riding in pulled up in front of American Airlines terminal to Los Angeles. The driver stopped the limo got out of the car walked around to DL's side, and opened the door. The driver called a skycap over to the back of the limo then directed the skycap to take out the luggage from the trunk. DL got out of the car he looked real bad, and was beginning to look pale.

DL started walking into the terminal he stopped turned, and looked at the door of the limo, his brother Joey stepped out of the car. He ran his hands into his pockets took out a wad of money then motioned to the skycap to come over to him. Joey gave him some money, looked over at DL nodded his head DL winked his eye, turned around and headed towards the terminal. He had started to peel out of his cloths he took off his black suit coat, and loosened his tie as he looked for a rest room. DL was beginning to feel nauseous. He entered the men's restroom and then headed for an empty stall. Once inside the stall he closed the door faced the toilet, and began to vomit blood. He began to feel better then flushed the toilet. After he came out of the stall, he made his way to the sink. DL turned on the water cupped his hands splashed the cool water all over his face. He turned off the water, and walked over to a wall near the exit door took some paper towels from the dispenser, and then dried his face off.

DL took a moment to take a good look at himself in the bathroom mirror. He didn't like what he saw. He really loved Jasmine, and it hurt him deeply that he had to put her to sleep the way that he did. While in a jealous rage he had lost control. He felt as though he had to save face in front of his family, it was all part of the game. He looked at his watch which read 2:30 a.m. He left the restroom then walked over to the bookstore near the boarding area, and bought a newspaper, pepto bismol tablets, and a Snicker's Bar. He paid for the items then headed towards the boarding area to Los Angeles. One of the flight attendants opened the door, and took a mic from the wall.

"Flight 402 to Los Angeles is now boarding" the flight attendant announced.

DL walked through the doors with all the other people. As he walks past one of the attendants, she noticed that he was sweating profusely and looked as if was just about to collapse.

"Sir! Are you all right?" the flight attendant asked.

"I'm fine, Thanks for asking" DL replied.

DL continued to walk down the corridor to the inside of the plane. He looked at his ticket as he searched for his seat, which was over the left wing. After he sat down he opened the package of Pepto Bismol. He popped a couple tablets in his mouth, and chewed them, as he looked out of the window of the plane. Dl noticed a tractor pulling a trailer with luggage on it below. The driver stopped jumped off of the tractor, to help the men put the luggage underneath the plane.

The attendant that took DL's ticket was standing in the kitchen area of the plane. They exchanged looks and smiled at each other from time to time, she felt attracted to him. As another attendant was setting up refreshments for the passengers they talked to one another as they giggled and looked in DL's direction. The plane was being readied for departure.

As the plane readied itself for takeoff one of the flight attendants reviewed safety instructions to the passengers. As she was checking seatbelts, the other attendant provided a damp cloth for DL since he was looking weak.

"Thank you what's your name sweetheart?" DL asked.

"Robin Fancies and yours?" she asked.

"DL . . ." he said.

"DL! What kind of name is that?" Robin said.

"If I tell you I'll have to kill you" he replied.

Robin was a 5'2" 90 pound cutie with brown skin light brown eyes, and full red lips. She was shaped like an hourglass. The curls in her hair encircling her beautiful face, it brought out the large dimples that appeared when she smiled. Robin looked at DL as if he was serious. DL returned her glance with a cold hard look, as if to say, he was not playing suddenly he broke out in a smile.

"I was just kidding with you sweetheart" DL Said.

"For a moment there I was beginning to believe you . . ." Robin said.

"Here, Take this thank you for helping me I want you to have a little something for you trouble" DL said.

DL reached into his pocket pulled out a wad of money and handed it to Robin who refused to accept it.

"DL, I cannot accept that from you I want to keep my job! But thanks anyway Can I get you water on ice?" the flight attendant asked.

"Sure, maybe it will calm my stomach down I feel nauseous and my head is killing me" DL replied.

"Sounds like flu symptoms to me are you taking good care of yourself? I'll be right back with some Alka-Seltzer and water" Robin said.

"OK, don't forget the ice" DL replied.

"I won't, now you just sit back and relax" said Robin.

After the signal rang the passengers took off their seat belts, and began to mill around talking to one another. Some passengers kicked back others read magazines or watched a movie. DL looked out of the window into the dark sky he looked down, and saw cars lights zipping through the city. Millions of lights sparkled like stars it reminded him of his trips to Disneyland when he was a child. As the plane glided through the air heading to Los Angeles DL opened his newspaper turned to the obituaries to read the article about Jasmine Cooper's death.

A little boy around six years old was playing with a toy gun two seats away. The child was dressed up like a cowboy. Wearing a brown and white cowboy hat, a white shirt brown and white vest jeans, and matching leather skins. On his feet he wore cowboy boots with spurs. His name was Darius he was on the ground crawling toward DL with a toy gun in hand. When Darius reached DL's seat he popped up over the arm of the chair next to DL, and then pointed his gun at DL.

"Stick em' up partner! And Hand it over!" Darius demanded.

DL played along with the little boy.

"I'm sorry, but I have no idea what you're talking about friend. Please don't shoot me, I'm unarmed what do you want?" DL asked the little cowboy.

"I saw you back at the airport in that book store buying a Snicker's I want it, and I want it now! No funny moves mister or I'll have to fill you with holes partner!" Darius demanded.

Just at that moment Darius mother approached him from behind grabbed his shirt, and then began scolding the little cowboy.

"Boy is you crazy! Is he bothering you sir?" asked the mother. "Darius, how many times have you and I talked about this? You cannot go around pointing guns at people! Now, I want you to apologize to the man" said the mother.

"He's alright ma'am, how old are you Darius?" DL asked the child.

"I'll be seven in two days. Mama's taking me to Knott's Berry Farm for my birthday. You want to come with us? It's going to be fun!" Darius said.

"I wish I could Darius but I have some very important business to tend to in Los Angeles. Here's a birthday present for you" DL said to the little cowboy as he handed him the Snickers candy bar.

Darius opened the wrapper took a bite of the candy bar, and while looking at DL the kid had a huge smile on his face.

"Thanks mister!" Darius said.

"You're welcome Darius" DL replied.

Darius and his mother walked back to their seats and DL returned to his newspaper article. Robin approached DL with a cup of water, and a package of Alka-Seltzer. As DL placed the tablets into the cup of water Robin prepared his tray for him.

"How very nice of you to do this! Since you won't accept money, can I Interest you in a nice dinner once we arrive in Los Angeles?" asked DL.

"Maybe, it all depends . . . . How do I know if you're not some kind of murderer or something like that?" asked Robin.

DL gave Robin a look, took a drink of his Alka-Seltzer, and then gave her that "you caught me" smile.

"You never know, however I do promise that you, and I will have a very good time together. I do know how to treat a lady, what do you say Robin?" DL asked.

"I have three days off when we get to LA. Sunday morning I have to be on the first flight back to Fort Worth . . . Here's my cell number use it before Saturday. Are you going to tell me what 'DL' means?" Robin asked.

"Let's see how the date goes. If you and I can get past first base on Saturday night, I'll tell you what the DL means Sunday morning" DL said.

# 2:45

It was Wednesday three days before the big day. It was 2:45 in the afternoon and the wedding party was in preparation for the Saturday's wedding ceremony. Sandy and her bridesmaids were all set for today's rehearsal. My best man Bernard and five of my frat brothers were paired off. Buddy Long with Moesha Jones, Deshawn Burton with Ann Davis, Michael Travis with Diamond Lewis, and Jim Wesley with Latonya Ferrell, and Braxton Toles with Victoria Adams. All of the couples were lined up at the front door waiting patiently for instructions from the wedding planner.

Mrs. Jefferson was a smart business woman who did things to perfection. Sandy and I were sitting at the front of the church waiting patiently, for our instructions. When everyone was in their places at the front of the church Sandy, and I were prepared to stand together with Pastor Williams. The bridesmaids and the groomsmen were to form a line from the left side of Sandy on the steps, down to the floor. Bernard and the groomsmen were to do the same thing forming a line from the right side of me to the floor. Everyone would end up facing one another.

The flower girl Sandy's young niece would carry a basket with rose petals. She was to walk down the aisle tossing rose petals on the floor as she made her way towards the Alter then take her place behind Sandy. As ring bearer my young nephew was to carry the wedding rings on a white satin pillow, then take his place behind me facing the flower girl. Mrs. Jefferson was in her late sixties

She was a very classy woman who loved jewelry, expensive wigs, tight jeans, colorful blouses, and high-heeled pumps. She looks pretty good for her age she had a smooth caramel brown complexion and she wore very little make up. All she required was a little foundation eyeliner, and a small amount of lipstick to enhance her beauty.

"Ok people, We want to look sharp this is a very special day for Jonathan and Sandy you are the wedding party, and you complement the bride and groom. When you walk down the aisle Dr. John Lehman will play Luther Vandross "Here and now" after you make your way to the front of the church, you are to quickly find your places. At that point Sandy and her father will walk down the aisle, as John continues to play. Sandy will end up at the top of the stairs with Jonathan and Pastor Williams. Are we all on the same page?" Mrs. Jefferson said.

"Yes, we're on the same page," the wedding party replied.

"Now, I think you're all ready for this Saturday. That's it for today ladies and gentlemen. I want you here at the church one hour before the wedding starts. This way you can help each other as you're all getting ready. Men, the same advice goes for you . . . I'll see everyone on Saturday." Mrs. Jefferson said as she gave her final instructions.

At 2:45 pm DL was admitted to St. Gabriel's hospital. Laying in a hospital bed with a tube in his mouth An I.V. was attached to his left arm with medication to treat what they thought to be the Swine Flu. The doctors stood around DL's bed talking as he lay in an unconscious state. After reviewing results of the many tests that were administered, they couldn't seem to find out what was making DL. Sick. Robin the flight attendant was waiting in the emergency room area and it had been four hours since he was admitted to the hospital. There was still no news regarding the cause of his grave condition. This made Robin very concerned about DL's health she was worried about him.

"Excuse me ma'am, Are you related to the gentlemen that you brought here this afternoon?" asked the doctor.

"No, I'm just a friend we met on the plane a few hours ago. Is he going to be alright?" Robin asked.

"Well, since you are not a relative, I can't tell you very much at this point, all I can tell you is that he is still unconscious" replied the doctor.

Our team of doctors took several tests and the results suggest the possibility that he may have the Swine Flu. All we can do now is wait to see how he reacts to the medication, and we hope that he wakes up soon. At that time we'll do more test and see what we come up with" the doctor said.

"Okay then when he wakes up, can you call me at this number? I am a stewardess for American Airlines I am staying at the Airport Hilton. I will be leaving on a flight for Dallas the day after tomorrow I'd like to know his condition before I leave" Robin said.

"Sure, I understand when we see a change in his condition someone will call you. However I do have a question for you? What did you notice about him before you brought him to the hospital? asked the doctor.

"Well, before we left Dallas I noticed he was sweating a lot and looked like he was about to faint. At that time I asked him if he was feeling all right. He told me had a splitting headache, and that he was feeling nauseous. After I gave him some Alka-Seltzer he appeared to be feeling better. Then when he got off of the plane he suddenly collapsed in the terminal" Sandy explained.

The doctor entered detailed notes in to his Blackberry as Sandy described DL's symptoms.

"One other question we looked in his wallet for some identification but there was nothing there. I understand he goes by 'D.L.'. Exactly what is the meaning of these initials? Asked Dr. White.

Robin smiled then told him what DL said to her.

"While we were on the plane I asked him the same question. He said, if he told me what those letters meant he would have to kill Me." said Robin as she smiled at the doctor.

"What? Come on! What kind of name is DL?" asked the doctor. "Those letters have to mean something!" he said to Robin.

Well, you know as much about him as I do. Please call me when you see a change in his condition" Robin said.

Robin walked away from the doctor strolled down the hallway. She stopped at the elevator looked back at the doctor they exchanged smiles. Robin entered the elevator then the doors closed. The doctor stood in the hallway with his hand on over his mouth with a perplexed look on his face. He shook his head walked to the nurse's station, and began looking at some charts. The Doctor looked at his Blackberry, and then picked up the hospital phone and dials a number.

"Hello, this is Doctor White over at emergency at St. Gabriel's. We have a patient here that has no identification we can't find any Information regarding his first or last name. This appears a little unusual, so I thought I would give you a call to see if there is a possibility that he may be someone you're looking for" said Dr. White.

Detective Stone was on the other end of the line. He hung up the phone, and walked over to the lab where Ericka was working on the Cooper case. The walls of the office were made of tinted glass. On the table where Erika was working was a computer touch screen that illustrated every picture that was taken at the Cooper crime scene. Erika worked diligently waving her hand in front of the screen repositioning, and enhancing pictures as she studied them.

"Look at the position of the gun on the floor. Now at the bullet hole on her forehead. It looks like he was standing at the foot of the bed and she was sitting up at the time when he pull the trigger. It appears as though he then walked around to the side of the bed to view her body, and then dropped the gun on the floor as he fled the crime scene" Erika explained.

"Did you find any prints on the gun?" inquired Detective Stone.

"Yes I did, come check this out" Erika responded.

Detective Stone and Erika walked over to a glass cubical station where a three sided computer screen sat on a desk. The program that was used to track down information on DL. Was the state of the art Integrated Automated Fingerprint Identification System also known as IAFIS. On one screen mug shots were scanned and the other two screens matched fingerprints. Erika enlarged a fingerprint that was taken from the gun used in the Cooper case. There was no match suddenly a picture of DL popped up along with everything else about him.

I just got off of the phone with a Doctor White over at St. Gabriel's he says they have a patient there who is unconscious; he says it might be someone we're looking for. He's been there since the early part of the day. And get this, he has no ID. Evidently he goes by the name of DL the same guy were looking for. You know it's kind of early in the morning could that be our DL guy? What time do you have?" asked Detective Stone.

"It's 2:45 am. You know, he just might be our guy" Erika said.

"This might be the break we've been looking for. Let's take a ride over to St. Gabriel's, and see if we can get lucky" Detective Stone said.

Detective Stone and Erika left the police station; they got into an unmarked car Ericka drove.

"Stone . . . I have a hunch that the guy at the hospital is the same guy responsible for the Cooper case, and the shooting at The Audition . . ." Erika said.

"It would really make my day if your hunch showed just a little validly to it. I would side with you but I am kind of on the fence with that theory, in a way. Each MO is different, in the Cooper case the victim was shot in the forehead with letters carved in her chest and then the killer left a weapon with prints. At the Audition the victim was shot point blank in the chest but the shooter left no weapon or evidence, he even took the shell casing from the bullet" Detective Stone said.

"I'm not feeling it Stone you might be wrong on this one. If I'm right, you have to buy me lunch every day until the end of the year. You have to buy me anything I want to eat, anywhere I choose. Deal?" Erika said.

"You don't know what you're getting yourself into Erika. You're forgetting, I have 16 years on the force, I think I know what I'm talking about. You only have seven years on the force you should listen to experience, like I did look where it got me," Detective Stone said. "I hear you, but I'm going to stick to my guns on this one. DL is our man" Erika said.

Erika pulled into the parking lot of emergency at St. Gabriel's then parked. Detective Stone and Erika got out of the car and they walk into the hospital. When they arrived at the front desk they asked to see Doctor White. Dr. White was in his mid-thirties' he was 6'0 185 pounds with a dark brown completion bald, and sported a neatly trimmed moustache with a neatly trimmed goatee. On his face he wore gold wire rimmed glasses made by Prada only to attract young females giving the false notation of his high intellect. He wore all white scrubs a pair of white crocks, and a stethoscope around his neck. Lookin' like a playa he entered through some lime green double doors to talk to Detective Stone. "I'm Doctor White are you Detective Stone?" Doctor White said.

"Yes, and this is my partner Detective Winston, do you have a patent here that goes by the name of DL?" Detective Stone asked.

"Yes, he was admitted early yesterday after about 2:45pm. A young lady brought him in. He was sweating and running a high temperature with stomach cramps. We did some test on him to see if he had the Swine Flu because he had all symptoms. We gave him a shot of the Swine Flu vaccine to combat the flu. One of my staff members noticed he became unresponsive after the vaccine. We had to put him on a respirator he wouldn't wake up. He's been that way all day, I'll take you to his room," Doctor White said.

DL had just awakened he saw all the tubes connected to his body. DL Looked around the room then took the respirator from out of his mouth and threw it on the floor. He sat up in the bed looked at the IV stuck in his arm, and ripped it out. He stood up on the side of the bed he felt a little dizzy but he was still able to function. He made his way over to the closet opened the door grabbed his cloths took off the hospital gown, and then put on his own.

Like a cat DL crept over towards the door opened it slowly stuck his head out into the hallway. No one was in the hallway so he ducked back in the room. DL peeked into the hallway again to see if it was clear then dipped out to the left, and swiftly down the hall to a stairwell. He exited the building walked to the front of the hospital grabbed a taxi, and they drove off. The doctor and the two detectives came walking from around the corner towards the room where DL was before they entered the room. Detective Winston noticed the door to the stair well closing as they were entering the room. The bed was empty Doctor White stepped into the hall way angrily calls the nurse. "Nurse! Nurse!" Doctor White said.

"Yes Doctor . . ." the nurse said.

"What happened to the patient that was in here?" the doctor asked.

"I don't know Doctor White, I just checked on him ten minutes ago, he was still unconscious," the nurse answered.

Erika took her gun out of its holster and headed toward the stairwell.

"Doc, where does this stairwell lead to? Erika asked.

"To the front of the hospital," Doctor White answered.

"We may still be able to catch him Erika you go down the stairwell, I'll take the elevators" Detective Stone said.

Detective Stone and Erika took off down the hallway in opposite directions in their attempt to catch DL. Detective Stone and Erika eventually met up in the front of the hospital without locating DL, no sight of him at all.

"That guy is good?" Erika said.

"We'll wait for him to surface again trust me he'll show up and when he does he'll get the surprise of his life" Detective Stone said.

# THE WEDDING

It was a clear beautiful Saturday afternoon a great day for a wedding. People were gathering in front of ST. Paul Lutheran Church along with the paparazzi. Every movie studio executive in Hollywood who was someone attended the wedding of Peter Zantex daughter, and soon to be son-in-law Jonathan Paul. I was about to marry the daughter of the most powerful man in the movie industry today. The news media had parked all along 9th Ave. to get first look or maybe get lucky with an interview from me, Supreme Studios' new secret weapon.

Peter Zantex was giving his daughter away today it looked like the 52nd Annual Academy Awards. Everyone was dressed in their finest St. Paul was filled with Hollywood's enquiring spectators. The church was filled with lavender rose petals that flowed through the center aisle leading to the altar. On each side of the aisle on the floor near each pew sat a small white candle. Suspended in the air were people dressed as angels with white satin gowns, and wings strapped to their backs. In each hand they held small pouches of White and lavender gold leaf stars ready to let it fall like rain at the end of the ceremony as the bride and groom exit the Church.

The church was packed Pastor ST. Williams Jr. Took his place at the altar. John Lehman the church choir director began playing Luther Vandross' "Here and now" as the bridesmaids and grooms began their walk down the aisle the guest were awaiting their arrival to enter the church. When they all walked down the aisle there were ooo's and ah's as the wedding parity made their way to the alter. Behind them came Sandy's niece and Jonathan's nephew. The bridesmaids were dressed in lavender satin dresses that came down in the front of their thighs just above their knees. The back of the dress fell down like a teardrop. The best man and my frat brothers were all dressed in White tuxedos with lavender cumber buns, and lavender bow ties.

Everyone gets into position from the top of the alter steps down to the bottom of the steps as rehearsed. I stood at the altar with Pastor Williams. Then came the moment that everyone was waiting for. Sandy and her father stood in the doorway at the back of the church looking at the altar. John Lehman began playing Arbil's "Love Me" Sandy looked so beautiful dressed all in white, she looked like an angel just sent from heaven.

Sandy wore a white satin asymmetrical layered dress that fits perfectly around her hourglass shape. On her head she wore a long white veil that covered her face then draped down to her elbows. Her veil was laced with small one-carat diamonds throughout the fabric concealing her beautiful radiant face. Around her neck she wore a serpentine diamond necklace with matching earrings. From her waist down the dress cascaded and flared out to a seven-foot train behind her. As she walked down the aisle it seemed as though she was floating across the floor.

Peter had the biggest smile on his face he was a proud father today soon that smile would turn into tears of joy. He was wearing the same thing that I was wearing with the exception of a lavender bow tie to complements his wife's dress. Today was the first day of the rest of our lives as one big RICH happy family. After today my prayers would be answered. Sandy and I were standing in front of Pastor Williams we looked at one another in agreement with the decision that we were about to make. By the look on Sandy's face you could tell that she loved the ground I walked on, and you could see the same look on my face as well, today I was the happiest man in the world.

"Jonathan and Sandy, I want to share something with you today. I want to the two of you to pay close attention to what the bible says about the permanency of marriage. And how it is a lifelong union. I'll share a passage with you both it's taken from Genesis. 'The Lord God said it was not good for a man to be alone, so He made a helper suitable for him for that reason a man will leave his father, and mother and be united to his wife, they will become one flesh" Pastor Williams said.

Sandy and I began to hold each other's hands as Pastor Williams continued to open our eyes to the new world that we are about to enter.

"If one of you begins to fall down be there to pick each other up. Today, God is joining the two of you together; always keep Him first in your lives. Jonathan, remember to keep God first, and then Sandy. It's a three cord relationship that God has put together" Pastor Williams said.

Sandy and I looked at each other then back towards Pastor Williams. I couldn't wait for the ceremony to end I was sweating, and feeling faint reality was starting to set in. After today I would be a married man. I only wished that my mother could have been here to see this day. My aunt was sitting in the front row crying her eyes out because she was thinking the same thing. It would have been a day of splendor for her sister to see her first born get married.

"Sandy, life is going to try to rip your head off, but you have to stay strong. Always ask God to give you strength, and He will see you through. It's hard to be obedient when bad things happen in your marriage. When these things happen take it to God, and He'll see you through it. Whatever the two of you go through give it to him he'll work it out for you, God is good" Pastor Williams said.

"All the time" The congregation responded.

Pastor Williams took a gold lavender, and white cord placed it over our heads to rested on our shoulders. The gold represented me the lavender represented Sandy, and the white represented God. The tri colored cord was a sign of our unity for life.

"As long as you stay close to Him your marriage will stay in a three cord union with God. A cord that no man on the earth can break" said Pastor Williams.

At that time Sandy's niece walked around and held up the satin pillow with my ring on top. At the same time my nephew did the same thing, I took Sandy's ring from the pillow, and the children returned to their places.

"Jonathan, do you take Sandy Zantex to be your wife, to love and cherish as long as the two of you shall live through sickness, and health until death do you part?" Pastor Williams asked.

"I do" I responded.

"And Sandy, do you take Jonathan to be your husband to love, and cherish as long as the two of you shall live through sickness, and health until death do you part?" Pastor Williams asked.

"I do" Sandy responded.

The paparazzi began to light up the church as they took pictures CLICK, SHISH, CLICK, SHISH as their cameras echoed against the walls of the church Sandy, and I began to exchange our wedding rings.

Sandy took my left hand slid the wedding band on to my left ring finger. It was gold trimmed in platinum. The entire band was imbedded with clusters of diamonds. The clusters of diamonds spelled out the initials J.P. When it was my turn I took Sandy left hand, and slid her wedding ring on her ring finger. It was also gold trimmed platinum, and resembled the Eiffel Tower. On top of the setting rest a gorgeous ten-carrot marquis diamond that would put your eyes out.

Now, is there anyone here that feels that these two should not be married? Speak now or forever hold your peace . . . With the power invested in me from God, I now pronounce you, Jonathan and Sandy man and wife. You can NOW, kiss your bride" Pastor Williams said.

Sandy looked at me we embraced one another then I gave Sandy a kiss that gave her that deep down gut feeling that made her know, how much I loved her.

"Congregation, I will now introduce to you Mr. & Mrs. Jonathan Paul" Pastor Williams said.

Sandy and I turned to face the congregation everyone stood to their feet and applaud in the union of our marriage. We walked down the steps towards the end of the church. As we made our way out of the church the angels that hung in the air scattered lavender, white and gold stars over our heads. We walked out of the church to an awaiting stretch white Bentley limousine. The driver of the limo opened the door for us Sandy got in first and I followed. Once inside the driver closed the door then returned to the driver's side, and we were in the wind. The wedding guests stood on the front lawn as they clapped, and cheered as we cruised down Adams in route to the reception.

Already in the parking lot of the Beverley Hills Hilton the news media was setting up to interview me. The paparazzi were outside of the entrance to the hotel awaiting a glimpse of the newly wedded Mr. and Mrs. Jonathan Paul. Supremes new mega-star. Some of the wedding guests had just arrived. The ballroom was setup with a live performing band, and a DJ. The tables were dressed with a white tablecloth and lavender napkins were placed to the left of each plate.

The finest crystal and silver were placed neatly on all the tables. It looks like a banquet fit for a king and his queen. Waiter's poured water into elegant glasses at each table. On the center of each table sat a beautiful arrangement of lavender and white roses in a glass vase trimmed with gold leaf. On the floor of the ballroom laid lavender and white rose petals.

Near the head table sat a mimosa fountain. Next to it was a beautiful seven layer white, and lavender wedding cake trimmed with gold leaf edible roses. The room filled with guests as the wedding party took their seats. Sandy's parents and my aunt sat across from our table. The DJ filled the air with smooth sounds that made the occasion a most memorable event.

Sandy and I just pulled up in the stretch limo, and the Paparazzi were on us like a glazed donut. The driver walks around to the rear of the limo to open the door for Sandy and I. Four huge bodyguards walked up to the car, then formed a human shield for us as we walked to the front entrance of the hotel. As we entered the hotel a news reporter yelled out my name. He wanted to interview me, but I wasn't feeling him at the moment. "JOHNATHAN! Can I get an interview from you before you go inside?" the reporter yelled.

Sandy smiled and encouraged me to speak with him.

"This will help your career do the interview go ahead talk to the man!" Sandy said.

As I stopped the human shield opened up, and the reporter walked through.

"Jonathan, I hear you're Supremes new secret weapon" the reporter said.

"I guess you could say that" I responded.

"What is the secret weapon?" he asked.

"Now, if I told you, it wouldn't be a secret anymore right?" I told him.

"How well did you know that public defender Jasmine Cooper, who was brutally murdered two weeks ago?" the reporter asked

"She was a very close and dear friend of mine," I said.

"Jonathan, is it true you had sex with her the night before she was murdered?" the reporter asked.

"ABSOLUTLEY NOT! We never had sex SHE WAS MY FRIEND!" I told him.

At that moment a huge bodyguard grabbed the reporter picked him up, and then slammed him to the ground destroying his camera, and then pushing the other reporter out of the way. Two of the bodyguards proceeded to expeditiously escort Sandy, and I to the awaiting reception.

"What in the hell was wrong with that guy? What's up with him asking me if I had sex with Jasmine? What the HELL! Was that all about?" I said aloud in exasperation.

"He was only doing his job Baby! COME ON! this is our wedding day! Don't let that bother you. You're my husband now I trust, and believe what you're saying about Jasmine. I know how you were with our relationship before we got married. I believed you when you said the two of you were not having sex. Baby just let it go this is our wedding day, don't let that get next to you" Sandy said in a loving voice.

"Today is our special day, and when I get you alone Baby it's goanna be on and crackin. I'm the one you're gonna have to worry about, come on we have guest waiting" Sandy assured me.

We walked into the ballroom where we were greeted with rounds of applause. We made our way to our table to join our wedding party. Sandy's father was conversing with the vice President of Supreme studios about a new project that I was staring in. Tony Hayden and Peter walked off towards the lobby together. Tony was a thin Jewish man in his early thirties with a salt and pepper beard cut close to his face. Average size built he was dressed in a black double-breasted suite a pair of black wing tips Stacy Adams, smoking on a cigar; he was a real hip kind of guy.

"This kid is going to make the studio a lot of money. He's smart he does his own stunts he's a second-degree black belt in martial arts and he also sings, the women will just love him. Remember back in the day when Hollywood was really Hollywood? And Elvis was signed to the studio at that time; He made Big bucks for the studio back then, GUESS WHAT? We're going to do the same thing with my son—in-law were going to make him a big star" Peter said.

"How long was their honeymoon planned for? We can start shooting with the B team next week I'm just saying" Tony said.

"Go ahead get your footage. By the time you're done, Jonathan should be back and ready to rock and roll. When were done with that film, we'll then crank out another one you feel me?" Peter said.

"Yeah Okay, I feel you I see what you doing. Back-to-back box office hits" Tony said.

"I'm going to make sure my grandchildren never have to work a day in their lives" Peter said.

Peter and Tony walked back into the ballroom. Bernard was standing in front of the band with a mic in one hand and a glass of champagne in the other.

"Can I have everyone's attention? For those of you that don't know me Jonathan, and I have been friends for a very, very long time. When we were in college we use to say that we would be each other's best man. Well, I've kept my promises Jonathan. Let's give a toast to my best friend, my frat brotha Omega Phi Nu fo life. Congratulations to the Paul's. May they enjoy a long life together, I LOVE YOU MAN!" Bernard said.

The photographers snapped pictures of the wedding party and of the bride and groom.

"Ok, this may not be in order but I want to see my brotha get that garter from under . . . well you know what I'm talking about. There's only one thing Jonathan, you have to do it blindfolded. DJ, give me a beat" Bernard said.

As Sandy's bridesmaids escorted me to the main floor the lights dimmed and the DJ started playing Nelley's "It's getting hot in here". Bernard set a chair down in front of me; Moesha a sexy Ethiopian exotic beauty made me kneel down then blindfolded me. After she helped me to my feet, she turned me around several times then lead me to the center of the floor. Sandy took a seat in the chair Moesha made me get down on all fours like a dog; I had to crawl on the ground on all fours to find my wife. Sandy called me then I headed towards her as I tried to get my bearings straight, and follow her voice because I was dizzy as hell. When I found her I lifted up her dress stuck my head under her dress and then removed her garter belt from her thigh with my teeth.

I stood up removed the blindfold I reached for my wife, and she threw herself into my arms. I took the garter belt from my mouth and tossed it in the air then kissed Sandy as the single men rushed to get it from the floor.

"Okay, we are going to slow it down a bit, and let the lovebirds do their thing on the dance floor. This song is for the bride and Groom" the DJ said.

Sandy and I took to the center of the ballroom floor as the DJ filled the room with music. He went old school with "Your My Everything" by the Delphonics. We danced our first dance together as man and wife in the center of the ballroom floor.

Something was about to go down on a yacht somewhere in the Florida Keys. In a room with red walls and sliding portholes in the center of the room was a mahogany rosewood conference table. At the table sat a large man in a black suit smoking a cigar. Around him were four green lamps hanging from the ceiling it gave off a soft light where the man couldn't be seen.

Nearby a man entered the room and headed towards the large man sitting at the table. As the figure moved closer the large man pushed a manila envelope towards him. The figure leaned forward with his left hand picked up the envelope and placed its contents on the tabletop. The large man seated at the table puffed on his cigar as the man picked up pictures of DL then returned them to the envelope. He moved into the light it was DL's brother Joey a two hundred twenty five pound weight lifter. He was an expert marksman could make a clean kill from a thousand yard away. No one could ever trace his shot he used a silencer on each job, and each one was as clean as the first. DL's father created animosity between the two brothers throughout their whole entire lives. Joey hated DL because he knew his father loved DL more than him. He felt that if he were given the chance he would knock DL out of the box. He would do this with no questions asked to prove just to his father that he was the better son. "Now you have the chance to show me what you are made of" the large man said.

Life has a way of bending you over and taking a giant plug right out of your backside. One evening a meeting was held at the big man's estate. Joey went to the wine cellar to get some wine. As he made his way down the stairs he heard some heavy breathing from a woman, and then some bumping around in the wine cellar. Joey slowly opened the door, and discovered DL having sex with his woman Jasmine cooper. Joey ended the relationship with her and never said anything about what he saw. It was just a matter of time until things would take care of themselves. Things would begin to change for Joey when all he wanted was to get revenge for the death of Jasmine Cooper. The tables had turned for DL, and his demise would come like a thief in the night.

Back at the reception Connie was talking to my aunt she's trying to get her to come out to Los Angeles to live. She needed someone to take over Sandy's job until she gets back from our honeymoon.

"What you need to do is to come live with me for a few months. I'm going to need some help around the studio until Sandy comes home from their honeymoon. Who knows, you may get lucky, and find yourself a man" Connie said.

"I guess I could do that, Jonathan has been trying to get me out here for the longest time. I had to come to his wedding. I'm his only living relative he's my sister first born. She passed when he was seventeen I'm all he has. I wouldn't have missed this for anything in the world" said Aunt Minnie.

"Girl, you won't have to worry about anything. While you're here you and I will look at some property, you're family now; we look out for one another? I got you girl!" Connie said.

Justin and his business partner were sitting at a table away from the family Justin was a little Jaded. David was concerned about Justin's wound, and was trying to get him into good spirits. "Are you alright?" David said.

"Just a little soreness in my shoulder, but I'm good" Justin said.

"Baby, do you want me to get you something to drink?" David asked.

"Look, kick back and let the waiters do their job" Justin replied.

Justin was somewhat bitter towards his father Peter. Justin would ask him to invest in his comic book business but his father always put him off.

"How much you think the old man dropped for this production?" Justin asked.

"About hundred thousand?" David said.

"Nope, NOT! Even . . . Try 2.5 Mill . . . See she's his firstborn and me; I'm just a bastard child. My mother ran off with the gardener. Peter just raised me, and took good care of me. But you see Daddy's little girl always gets whatever the fuck she wants. This bastard only gets nothing but a lesson learned" Justin said.

"What lesson did you learn Justin?" David asked.

Your mom's is your porthole into this fucked-up world. When her job is done she leaves you with someone who will take care of you until you're ready to do everything for yourself. You grow up real fast, and then you forced to learn how to deal with things only to make your own decisions in life. Get put on hold because they are too fucking busy to help you with your career only to end up like you and I, broke as a joke, and riding on other people's coat tails of success" Justin said.

"Why are you so anger Justin? You have you're comic book it's about to drop. Soon your ship will come in. I wouldn't worry myself with all that bullshit, Honey Success is goanna find you!" David said.

"Yeah rite . . . We'll see we shall SOON SEE . . ." Justin replied. As he glairs at his sister and Jonathan while they were taking pictures with the wedding party.

The wedding parity was standing outside near a waterfall. Sandy, Connie, Peter, Aunt Minnie and I stood around talking to each other while the photographer prepared to take our pictures.

"Okay Family. Everyone look at me. Smile on three. Five, Four, Three . . . click, click, click . . . That's it, that's what I'm talking about!" the photographer said as he worked.

# WATCH YOUR BACK

L was in his downtown loft resting across his bed he wasn't feeling good at all. His loft was neatly tucked away from the main street. The only way to get to it was from Seventh Street down in a dark alley. DL was in bad shape he had sores all over his face and arms. Swiftly DL got up from his bed went to the rest room and started coughing up blood this time couldn't stop. He stood over the toilet to compose himself then he spit out the remaining blood from out of his mouth. His lips were sore and severely swollen. DL flushed the toilet then walked over to the sink ran some cold water. He leaned over into the sink to rinse out his mouth. He looked at himself in the mirror, and didn't like what he saw. Something was wrong, and it wasn't the Swine Flu.

He looks down at his hands they looked like worms were crawling underneath his skin. He looked in the mirror and noticed same thing happening to his face. He started screaming because of the excruciating pain he was experiencing. Suddenly DL began to play back in his mind everything he had done in the past week. For the past two days his memory was a little fuzzy he thought back to when he was at the club. The only thing he could remember was when the waitress brought the drinks to the pool table, she set them down then he remembers trying to get her phone number.

Suddenly he remembered that the waitress kept looking behind him. He was so into trying to get her number that he didn't turn around to see what she was looking at. DL grabbed his coat entered his elevator where his 300 was parked. He got into his car started the engine and slowly the elevator began to descend down to the alley. When he reached the ground floor he pulled off with the 1X-LOVER license plates in view. DL zoomed off down the alley turned left on 7th street to Broadway, made left on 5th street then hit the Harbor freeway north bound to the club. DL pulled into the parking lot of the Audition and parks. DL gets out of his car then made his way into the club. Standing in the doorway of the club DL looks around for the waitress he saw her across the room she was talking to the bartender. DL walks over to where she was standing.

"Excuse me can I talk to you a moment?" DL Said.

She turns to talk to him, and then suddenly drops the trey she was carrying. The waitress saw sores all over his face it kind of shook her up a bit. DL took her over to a table near the back of the club they sat down.

Gerald was sitting at the bar having a drink. He overheard DL talking with the waitress. Gerald casually got up from the bar with his drink, and walked over to a video game near their table. He put in some coins took a seat, and started playing a game. From where he was sitting he was able to see, and hear everything they said.

"Are you alright? Can I get you something to drink?" the waitress asked.

"No thanks I'm good. I need to know something? When I was here two days ago playing pool with that guy . . . Shene, yea Shene . . . you were looking past me at him, what was he doing?" DL asked.

The waitress gave him a look as if she didn't know what he was talking about. She didn't want to get mixed up into any mess. DL reached into his coat pocket pulled out a tan envelope then laid it down on the table while looking at her. The waitress looked at the envelope then looked at him. Gerald looked up from time to time, and then back at his game, DL's back was facing Gerald. He was running out of coins so he got up walked over to the bartender got some change, and refreshed his drink then got back to the video game, and continued playing his game.

"Look, I don't want to be mixed up in anything that will come back to haunt me, you know what I mean?" the waitress said.

"I do, you see my face? Look at my arms! It feels like worms are eating me alive I'm in a lot of pain. I'm coughing up blood and its getting worst. I went to the hospital yesterday and they can't find anything wrong with me. If you know something please tell me" DL begged.

DL slid the envelope towards the waitress but kept his hand on it. Gerald took out his iPhone without anyone knowing and took several pictures of DL and the waitress at the table talking. Gerald sent the picture to me along with a text.

"It feels like I'm dying . . ." DL said.

"Let's see now, after I set the drinks down on the pool table you and I were talking. I saw him go into his pocket and took out what looked like a small medicine vile. It looked like the kind the nurse puts blood samples in but it was smaller. It had some green liquid in it. Then it looked like he poured it into your drink then and walked away. I wasn't sure if that was what I saw now that I'm talking to you, that's what I remember seeing," the waitress said.

DL took his hand off of the envelope. The waitress picked it up opened it then looked inside.

"Ten thousand dollars! This is a lot of money! How do I know the information I just gave you won't go any further than this table?" she asked.

"You have my word I'm a businessman it will not go any further than this table, you can trust me" DL said as he coughed.

"Oh my God! You're coughing up blood! Here take these napkins, Wait here I'll be right back" the waitress said.

The waitress left the table and walked over to the bar got DL a glass of water and more napkins.

"Here drink this WHAT! Are you going to do? You need to get that taken care of soon. That doesn't look good you're coughing up to much blood dude!" the waitress said.

"I know it doesn't, we all have to die someday right? The person that did this to me I'll hunt him down like a dog. You can trust me on that baby girl believe that! Thank you" DL said.

DL got up from the table touched the waitress' hand then made his exit out the back door of the club. The waitress called out his name he stopped to hear what she had to say.

"DL, there's more yesterday some guys were in here looking for you. They talked to the bartender and a few other people. They were showing your picture around and asking questions" the waitress said.

"What did they look like?" DL asked.

"The guy that was asking about you looked like a weightlifter. I noticed he had a scar on the left side of his face" the waitress said.

"That's sounds like Joey! Hum, I wonder what that was all about!" DL said.

DL and the waitress sat at the bar for a long time talking. "I was standing a few feet away from them and I heard the big guy say, 'I have been waiting to do this for a long time. When I pull the trigger he'll never know what him'. DL you better watch your back looks like they mean business" the waitress said.

"Is that right? Okay, NOW this is personal. He wants to play like that ok don't worry I got this baby girl. You've been a great help, and thanks for the heads up" DL said.

DL walked out of the back door to the parking lot the waitress took the envelope put it in her pocket then went back to work. Gerald's phone began to ring It was me calling him. In nonchalant way he got up from the video game and walked outside to take the call.

"How does it feel to be a married man?" Gerald asked.

"Brotha, it feels good I am blessed to have a wife like Sandy. She keeps me grounded we are having the time of our life here in Paris. I'm really digging this marriage thing man. Hey Dog, what's up with those pictures you sent me. I know the girl she's the waitress at The Audition but who's the guy in the picture?" I said.

"The guy in the picture is DL what did you do to him? I mean what did Shene . . . you know what hell I'm trying to say. What did ya'll do to him? Whatever you did that brotha is not happy about it" Gerald explained.

"Well the other day when you and Bernard hooked me up with that latex I went to the club that night and we kicked it. He and I played a little pool, then I ah . . . Well let me put it this way we had a drink together, and that's all I'm gonna say about that" I told him.

"Well, the cat is out of the bag now. The waitress told him she saw Shene put . . ." Gerald said.

"Yo Dog! Check this out! We'll talk about it later, some things you just can't talk about over the phone Dog" I said.

"I feel you . . . but dude, he looks like a monster he has these open sores all over his face and hands he looks like he's got leprosy or something. It was nasty looking! Jonathan on the real man you better watch your back" Gerald said.

"You mean Shene right? He doesn't know anything about me" I told him.

"Check this out She also said some guys came in the club yesterday lookin' for him. I think they want him real bad" Gerald said.

"Dude! Why you trippin!" I said.

"My bad, I'm just concerned about you Jonathan you my Ninja we have to look out for one another" Gerald said.

Paul Higgins

"Good lookin out. This is what I need you and Barnard to do while I'm gone. I need a full size human like body with Shene's face on it and I'm gonna need a rigged up muscle car" I said.

"Okay, we can do that it's a done deal. All right then we'll talk later enjoy the rest of your honeymoon man, and be safe. Tell Sandy I said 'hey girl'" Gerald said before he hung up.

I have another trick up my sleeve Shene would be written out of the script in order for me to make some real movie magic. You know Sometimes we can get to attached in situations, and the results can end up affecting a lot of people's lives in a negative way. We have to be mindful of the ground where we choose to do are battle's on. I'm a married man now everything I've prayed for has been given to me with no question asked. So now I must do my part by do the right thing so that Sandy and I can continue receiving God's blessing. I have to think of my new family and my future. I can't throw it all away behind my own selfish gain. I've worked too hard to allow myself to crash, and burn. But you know what it ain't over until fat lady sings.

# THE DECOY

The honeymoon was over and everything was working out between Sandy and I. The production company with Bernard and Gerald was coming along very well. Our company would supply every movie studio, and Production Company in the world with our human-like latex skin. My company also worked with robotics, and computer technology which is my field of profession. Our company also known as HLLS Inc., was now ten days old Sandy would run the business while Gerald and Bernard made sure the HLLS Inc. products would get out to companies that needed our survives. She made sure to deal with all the customers while I dealt with the technological part of the company.

I was in my office sitting at a desk hooking up a new virtual driving program to my computer. The program would allow me to see things as though I was actually there. A human-like robot would link into my system. So whatever a person did; the robot would mirror every movement activated by their body heat. Whatever the robot saw I would see the same thing in real time. This program would be connected to a satellite in space so whatever big brother could see; I was able to see as well. Suddenly, there was a knock at the door.

"Hey Jonathan do you have a minute? Gerald and I would like for you to see something. I think you're going to like this," Bernard said.

I got up from my computer workstation and followed them out of the office. They walked down the hall to the right. Bernard opened a door, and we all walk in. In-the center of the room sat a decoy it was a human like robot, with the likeness of Shene. He wore a black tight knit T-shirt, black jeans some black biker boots, and some dark sunglasses. Bernard took a remote control box from the table next to him, and gave me a demonstration. Bernard turned on the remote then told me to walk in front of the decoy. I leaned forward to look in the decoy's face it looked back at me in the same way. As I tilted my head from side to side the decoy mimicked my every movement. I moved to the left of the robot, it followed me with the same head movement.

"Watch this Jonathan; Are you ready to work Shene?" Bernard asked

Shene nodded his head in agreement with Bernard.

"This is to cool man; I knew you guys could do it. That's why Supreme keeps you pot heads on their pay roll" Jonathan said.

"Look who's talking . . . we have something else to show you. It's right outside" Bernard said.

They walk out of the building and Parked on the side was a black 2012 Ford Cobra Shelby GT 500 GR with a short block 7.0 hemi engine on low profile racing tiers, and black tinted windows.

"Get in Jonathan! Start her up!" Gerald said.

I got in and cranked her up the engine sounded like a funny car. I closed the door and put on the seatbelt. I gunned engine twice it had so much power I couldn't believe it. This time I put it in drive and hit the brakes and gunned the engine once more. The car raised up as the tires spun out Blue smoke filled the air while sounding off like a mad lion. I put the car in park and listened to the engine as the motor loped in perfect timing it was time to rock and roll.

"Man! This is a monster! I should keep this car for myself" I said.

"You said you wanted a muscle car. Well, there she is! A Shelby GT 500 Gr with dual overhead cam supper charged 7.0 with a little twist to it. And check this out; she can do 0-60 mph in 4.0 sec" Bernard said.

"Damn! Well alright, let's do this Gerald while I pair the computer and the robot together, you call the club ask the bartender if DL is there if he is Shene wants to talk to him" I said.

Bernard and I brought the decoy to the car. We put him inside strapped the seat belt on then close the door. We all walked back to the office I saw Gerald talking on his phone he appeared to be talking to the bartender at the club. I sat down at my computer put on my head visor started the program then cranked up the monster. I put it in drive and the car took off down the lot and then on to the street heading toward the Club. The car pulled up into the parking lot facing the back of the club, I parked it with the engine still running.

"The Audition this is Rudy speaking, May I help you?" Rudy asked.

"Rudy, this is Gerald Baby let me ask you something . . . There's a cute guy that comes in there from time to time he goes by the name of DL, have you seen him today by any chance?" Gerald said.

"Baby, he's sitting right in front of me as we speak I'll let you talk to him" Rudy said.

Gerald gave me the phone.

"Who is this? DL asked.

"Your worst nightmare Shene Hilton" Shene said.

"Is that right? Well, let me ask you something is this business or is it personal?" DL asked through his cough.

"It's personal my brotha. You took something away from me so I'm returning the favor. Your reign of terror will soon end, It's only a matter of time" Jonathan said.

"What friend are you referring to?" DL said.

"How soon do we forget Jasmine Cooper doesn't that name ring a bell? Let's handle this on the street I'm parked in the back of the club you'll see me; I'm in a black Cobra GT 500 GR. You like to take lives I see, so come try to take mine, if you think you can . . . POTNER!" I said.

"You ain't said nothing but a word . . . Game on!" DL responded.

DL walked out of the back door of the club then stopped dead in his tracks when he saw the black Cobra at the end of the parking lot. Bernard, Gerald and I could see D.L on the computer screen. I gunned the engine and the whole front end rose up like it was breathing as the Cobra inched forward in an intimidating way.

DL made his way over to his 300 Charger got in and started his engine. The two cars were facing one another slowly the cobra moved forward as the engine roared. It pulled up alongside of DL then stopped. The window rolled down slowly as the decoy was looking forward then he turned his head to looks at DL. I continued to gun the engine. DL strapped himself in with his seat belt gunning his 660 Hemi engine while putting on black gloves.

Then I floored it! The decoy made a hard right onto La Cienega ripping down the street weaving in and out traffic. DL was dead on him the decoy was approaching Wilshire when the traffic light turned red. I down shifted and turned left almost hitting two oncoming cars. DL stopped to let two cars pass he turned left burning rubber to catch up with the decoy. By that time he was flying down Wilshire Boulevard the decoy turned left onto Crescent Heights and proceeded north up Crescent Heights. DL was starting to get dizzy he made a hard left turn onto Crescent heights side swiping cars and flooring it.

The decoy shot across Santa Monica Boulevard making four cars slam into one another. DL couldn't follow because four cars were blocking the enter section of Crescent Heights and Santa Monica. DL turned left almost hitting a man walking his dog. He swerves around the pedestrian almost hitting him, and continued speeding down Santa Monica Boulevard. The decoy turned left onto Sunset Boulevard flying he was going so fast it looked like the moving cars were standing still while weaving in and out of traffic like a racecar driver.

Doheney was right up ahead an island would appear in the center of the road where two streets merged into one another. It's where Tower Records use to be. The decoy was zooming down sunset when DL merged with the decoy they slammed into one another. DL tried to run the decoy off the road to the right was a parked tow truck with a bed sitting in the decoy's path. I had to think fast, so I made the decoy drive the Cobra up the ramp and on to the back of the tow truck sending the Cobra airborne. It took off like a jet then landed hard onto the pavement the decoy was off and running. DL slammed into two cars making them move out of his way in pursuit of the Cobra out of nowhere two police cars took off after DL.

"Dispatch, can you run these plate for me 1X-LOVER?" the police officer said.

"1X-LOVER Texas Plates, Registered to a Darlan Lover. There is warrant out for his arrest for the murder of Jasmine Cooper. He is armed and dangerous approach with extreme caution" replied the dispatcher.

"Put your seat belt on partner looks like this is going to get a little ugly" said the police officer.

The police were right behind DL while the decoy was flying down sunset. As he came to a curve I down shifted to second. On my way out of the curve I hit the virtual gas pedal the Cobra was gone and the police were not far behind. DL tried to ram the decoy in the rear so I down shifted and then pulled away. Up ahead was the 405 Freeway onramp I made a hard right then took off flying on the freeway. Overhead flew a police helicopter keeping track of every move the decoy and DL made.

DL made a right turn taking part of a fence with him. The decoy was weaving in and out of traffic, burning up the road. Suddenly they were side by side looking at one another. I made the decoy rammed the side door of the passenger side of the Charger. DL rammed me back I down shifted to slow down then cut to the right, I hit the nitrous Oxide button the decoy was out of there like a bat out of hell leaving DL and the Police far behind.

As the decoy approached Mulholland Drive I started breaking it down so the decoys could make a sharp right turn. Committing to the right turn while drifting around the corner about a block down I made a sharp left turn picking up speed and put it down. The decoy looked into the rear view mirror and through his eyes I could see two sets of bright neon headlights moving closer and closer. Suddenly the police helicopter appeared and shot past the Cobra overhead. It then hovered over the road level with the Cobra they were face to face. Using the On Star on board of the Cobra I typed in a code shutting the helicopter engine down.

"May-Day, May-Day we're losing power, we're going down we have to end pursuit . . ." the chopper pilot said.

The front of the helicopter dipped downward, then lifted up, it stalled swayed to the right nose-diving into a cannon crashing into the hillside.

"We lost the bird we need another one in the air. These guys have some serious muscle under their hoods; we need some back up out here. We're heading east on Mulholland Drive see if you can get a roadblock ASAP at Mulholland and Coldwater Canyon" the police officer said.

"Rodger that . . . air support on its way" the dispatcher replied.

The decoy came to a corner I down shifted to second turning out of the curve flooring it. DL was right on my bumper; he sped up alongside of the decoy ramming the passenger side of the car real hard almost pushing the decoy off the road. I broke it down again then gave it gas leaving DL in the dust once more. Up ahead were two police cars blocking off Coldwater Canyon. There was a four-foot gap between the two police cars as they faced one other. I stopped the decoy then revved up the engine, in the rear view mirror I could see DL coming around the bend really fast. I slapped the gear shifted into first burning rubber then took off. After gaining up enough speed I turned the virtual wheel to the left then quickly to the right using the hill like a ramp. The left front and rear tire were up in the air. The decoy was driving on two wheels sideways right between the two police cars past the roadblock landing and on all four tires. I gunned the engine while spinning the tires creating heavy blue smoke, the decoy was off and running ripping down the highway.

The police that were standing in the middle of the street were amazed at how that car got past them. They heard another car speeding towards them they looked at each other, and dove to the side of the road to keep from being hit. DL blew right past them hitting the two parked police cars knocking them out of commission. The other two police cars were still in pursuit trying to keep up with DL. The decoy was flying while drifting in and out of each curve. Up ahead a water mane had burst in the middle of the road I saw the water, and started to slow the monster down when it began to hydroplane into a spin.

I tried to hold it together to keep from slamming into the side of the hill, DL does not slow down. With the front end of his car he smashed into the driver's side of the decoy, pushing it until the Cobra fell off the side of the cliff. The decoy and the car fell eight hundred feet down the side of the hill, and then burst into flames. DL came to a full stop saw smoke and smoldering flames, he smiled then sped off down the hill.

The Police stopped to see if they could save the driver with no luck they called for the paramedics and rescue a team. I intercepted the call, and sent some actors dressed up like paramedic and rescue workers to tie up all the loose ends. I got out of the driving simulator removed the virtual driving head set.

"DAMN! I hated to wreck that car. It really felt like I was driving that monster. Woo! Okay check this out our second team is on their way to get the robot and the car, in a few days we are going to Shane's funeral" Jonathan said.

I got a call from one of our frat brothers Jim who was in charge of bringing the car and the robot back to the studio.

"Hey Jonathan, We have the car! And guess what? Your robot was intact" Jim said with excitement.

"What do you mean 'the robot is intact'?" I inquired.

"The Cobra is toast the only damage to the robot is burnt cloths. The fire didn't touch the face or body at all" Jim said.

"That's good to know, Hmm . . . All right I'll talk to you later call me when you're on the lot, I want to see what you're talking about" I said.

I shut my phone off put it in the holster, and took a seat at my computer in shock.

"Gerald, call New World Casting and tell them we need a one hundred non-union extras for a funeral shoot at Forest Lawn this Friday at 1:00 pm. Tell them everyone is to wear black. I need eight union extras one to play a pastor, and the rest to play family members" I said.

Gerald immediately got on the phone and called New World Casting.

"Bernard, guess what Jim just told me? The robot survived the crash, and the fire did nothing to the latex. I think Gerald may have landed all of us on a gold mind with his HLLS" I said.

"Okay Jennifer, Thanks they can all meet at the gravesite, yea Forest Lawn. Oh, and tell them all to be there thirty minutes before their call time and come camera ready. This Friday 1:00pm. That's it one hundred extras, Non-union, Pastor—union and seven family member's. Okay, thanks" Gerald said.

"What are you girls talking about? Cant' you whisper? I heard everything ya'll said" Gerald told them.

"Don't say anything Bernard, What were we talking about then? What? I can't hear you!" I said.

"Jonathan, you of all people need to stop. I'm not feeling you today all that mess you're talking about, you can miss me with that shit" Gerald replied.

"Wow, aren't we touchy today! Man I'm just playing with you" I said to Gerald.

"He got funky with you after he got off of the phone. I know him, he's not mad at you. Something else is wrong with him, GERALD what's wrong man?" Bernard asked.

"Yesterday my lover and I broke up. When I was talking to Jennifer I heard his voice in the background talking to this guy name Sonny. He hangs around the club . . . now I know why he was acting funny with me. He's seeing Sonny . . . I knew he was cheating on me" Gerald said.

"Man, don't trip off of that something better will come along. When God closes one door another one opens, so don't even worry about it" I told Gerald.

"Your right, I'm sorry for snapping at you, so what were you about to tell me?" Gerald said.

# WAKE UP CALL

As I made my way home I stopped by Starbuck's to get two caramel mochas. I figured Sandy and I could spend some chill time together tonight. When I got home I would turn on the fire place then Sandy and I could cuddle up on the couch and check out a real good DVD. I entered Starbuck's and place my order. Over In the corner of the store sitting at a table was a little old lady drinking a plain cup of hot coffee, and reading a book. Periodically she would look up and stare at me, soon my order was ready. After I paid for the two coffees I turned around and started to walk out of the store. Suddenly the little old lady stops me before I get to the door.

"Young man May I talk to you for a moment?" the old lady said.

I stopped to listen to the Lady.

"Would you mind sitting with me for a moment? I would like to share something with you if I could" the old lady said.

I took a seat across from her and noticed a cold glare in her eye. She looked at me as though she knew me. The lady laid her book down on the table, the book cover read: "Who Listens to Their Guardian Angel" she looked directly into my face then began to open my eyes regarding my spirit, and blessings to come, she kind of gave me the creeps.

"You're a Christian man Jonathan and God has blessed you. He wants you to do something for Him in order for Him to continue blessing you" she said to me.

"How do you know my name?" I replied.

"That's not important, God sent me here to tell you something" she continued.

It took a lot for me to sit and listen to what this stranger had to tell me, but I realized that this was a real wake up call for me, and that I should hear her out so I stayed and listened to her.

"What happened to Jasmine . . . was meant to be, she was called home because her mission here on earth was complete, and God wanted her home. I know you cared for her but this is not your fight. You have a mission to complete for God Jonathan. He has blessed you with your hearts desirers. Your mission is to do just that . . . He will deal with DL for what he has done, let me share something with you" the old lady said.

The old lady reached into her pocket and pulled out an old tattered bible. She began to thumb through the pages to find a message for me; she turns to Isaiah 34:8 and began to minister to me.

"This is the plan that was set forth to us about judgment against the nations. For the Lord has a day of vengeance. There will be a year of retribution to uphold Zion's cause. He will fight your battles for you. Jonathan you must repent and go to DL ask for forgiveness. Then you must turn what you have done around in order to continue to receive God's blessings. The Father understands the way you feel, repent then move on with your life with your new family Glory be to God" preached the old lady.

This was so strange, but I understood everything the little old lady was saying to me. I held my head down knowing what I had to do, and thought about what if DL Kill's me. It didn't matter I had to make a change to keep receiving God's blessings. When I looked up to thank the little old lady she suddenly appeared to me as my own mother.

"Jonathan I love you so much. I wanted to tell you that before God called me home. I want you to know that I'm with you always; you can talk to me through your heart. I have not gone anywhere, you and I will always be connected forever, and yes I do approve of your wife, she reminds me a little of myself. Jonathan, Baby you need to do the right thing. Remember what I taught you . . . What I taught, YOU! Remember?" she said to me.

The likeness of my mother suddenly disappeared. It was as if no one had ever been sitting there at all. I had just received a revelation I decided then it was time for me to make a change in my life. I got up from the table picked up the two coffees and strange enough they were still steamy hot. I exited the door, and walked to my car. Suddenly the sky turn dark grey then clouds rolled in overhead, as I got into my car, I begin to pray.

"Most gracious heavenly Father I come to you with an open heart and open mind. I poisoned a man out of anger; he took a life of a good friend from me. Father I'm asking for your forgiveness for what I have done. Father, I have to ask this man to forgive me for what I have done to him that's not the way I was taught. I also ask you to soften his heart so that we can make this right, before it's too late. Tonight I could lose my life but I must make this right to keep receiving your blessings so I give it all to you. My life is in your hands heavenly Father, hear my prayer. All these things I ask to be done through my Lord and Savior your son Jesus Christ. Amen, Amen and Amen" I prayed.

The moment I ended my prayer, a loud thundering sound rang out from the skies. Flickering light dancing all across the sky as the rolling thunder sound dissipated. The sky became calm and a bright beautiful day appeared once again. I picked up my phone from the passenger seat looked through the address book, and pulled up Jasmine's number. I began to dial the number.

"Hello . . ." I heard DL's voice say.

"My name is Jonathan Paul I was a friend of Jasmine Cooper's. Am I speaking with Darlan Lover AKA DL?" I said into the phone.

"It might be . . . What I can do for you" DL said in reply.

"Can you and I meet somewhere? There is something you, and I need to talk to about, I think I can help you" I said.

DL was coughing so bad I could hardly understand him. "What do you and I have to talk about?" he asked.

"Look, we are wasting time here meet me at the Audition Club in a half an hour. Your life depends on it" I told DL.

I hung up the phone started my car and then headed for the club. Two things were about to happen DL could kill me or we could both go home. I pulled up into the parking lot of the Club parked my car, and then entered the club. As I entered through the back of the club I started looking around to see if DL was there yet. I didn't see him so I sat at the end of the bar where I could see who entered the club. I took out a cigarette lit it, and then ordered a Green Apple Martini. The bartender set the drink down in front of me as he picked up the money then walked away. Just then DL came walking through the door. He could barely catch his breath. The sores on his hands and face had gotten worse. He walked over to a table near a wall across from where I was sitting at the bar as DL took his seat, he looked up and we locked eyes.

I got up from my seat with my drink and walked over to where DL was sitting. I sat down across from him and yes I was nervous as hell we were finally face to face. I sat my drink down on the table while smoking the last of drag of my cigarette. I looked at him and then the put my cigarette out in the ashtray on the table. DL was weak but I knew he could still do a lot of damage. I knew he wanted to hear what I had to say; DL looked at my drink raised one eyebrow, and then looked at me with an unsure look on his face.

"What do you want to talk about?" DL asked.

"Your condition, I'm the one to blame for that. You took a close friend away from me, and I'll never see her again. I wanted to do you the same way you did her only slower. I wanted you to suffer but you know what? I would be no better than you, if I let you die. Remember when you played pool the other night? Green Apple Martini Shene . . . Hilton? Remember? Well, you didn't know at the time it was me. I slipped eight grams of anti-freeze in your drink now it's only a matter of time now" I explained to DL.

"Why are you telling me this? You know I have taken so many lives; another one will not make a difference, it's all business with me. That's how I make my living, what happened with Jasmine? She was an informant, MY WIFE. A lot of people died behind what she did don't get me wrong, I did love her but I was ordered to take her out. In the event it was not done they were going to take my life as restitution, what could I do?" DL said in a weak voice.

"You also shot my brother in-law Justin point blank in the chest but he's going to be alright. You have ruined a lot of people's lives but you know what? People can change; I believe people deserve a second chance. I said all of that to say this now that you know the truth, you can kill me if you want but before you do that, I need your forgiveness for what I did to you what I did was wrong. Can you forgive me for what I have done?" Jonathan said.

Just then a sense of calmness came over DL that he had never felt before. For the first time in his life he felt remorse for all the lives he had taken. For a man to come to him and then ask for his forgiveness filled a gap of emptiness in his soul. He too wanted to turn his life around but was it too late for him?

"What's your name man?" DL asked.

"Jonathan Paul" I replied.

"Well Jonathan, I have a lot of respect for you to have come and ask for my forgiveness for what you had done to me. In any other situation you would have been dead a long time ago for sure, to come and tell a man what you just told me. You would be pushing up daisies as we speak. You want me to forgive you for what you've done to me right? Well, I guess I can. Can you forgive me for all the bad things I've done?" asked DL.

"Yes my brotha, I can forgive you and God loves you. Look, there's a doctor in Paris who is a friend of mine he can reverse what's happing to you, but we need to get you out of the country undetected. You know there are lots of people who are not very happy with you right now. One group wants you in prison and the other group wants you dead. You know I can be in a lot of trouble for helping you right? I'll help you but we need to leave right away so the doctor can cure your terminal illness. You have about forty-eight hours left after that your life is over then its toast for both of us if you know what I mean" Jonathan replied.

"Why are you doing this Jonathan?" DL asked.

"Because I'm a Christian and we are all God's children. We are supposed to love one another, I am my brother's keeper my brotha. This was a wakeup call for both of us. I have to do the right thing in order to keep getting my blessings Trust me God has really been good to me, I have to do the right thing and so do you . . . Be ready to leave tomorrow night there's something we have to do first so we can get you out of the country safely. Come to this address after midnight and don't be late" I said.

DL got up to leave but before he left he shook my hand. We walked toward the back door, and then just as D.L started to exit the club Joey and three goons stopped him at the back door.

"I think you and I need to talk Big Brotha" said Joey.

One of them grabbed DL and slammed him up against the wall. I ran over to help DL and blocked a right hand punch from Joey then shoot a right hand punch to his solarplex knocking the wind out of him. Then I delivered a wild left cross to his face sending him back into the other goons knocking them all down like bowling pins. I helped DL to his feet and stood in front of him in an on guard stance waiting for their sudden attack. Joey and his goons picked themselves up from the ground that's when Joey ordered the three men to kill me.

"What that hell you waiting for KILL HIS ASS!" Joey ordered.

They all surround DL and I, the goon on DL's right pulled out a gun. I side stepped to his right grabbed the goon's right hand, and then crossed it over with my left hand smashing the living day lights out of his face with the gun. With my right leg I did a reverse backspin kick to the other guy's head knocked him out cold. Now Joey and one other person were standing in front of me they made an ill-advised move towards me.

I jumped up in the air, and with my right leg kicked the guy to my left in the face knocking him to the ground. Before I put my foot on the ground I slapped Joey in the face with the same foot sending him to the ground like a sack of potatoes, then he scrambled for his gun. While I was concentrating on Joey, I got hit in the jaw by one of the goons. Without haste DL whipped out his gun and shot Joey in the hand that stopped him in his tracks, as the gun fell to the ground. Slowly the badly beating cronies one—by—one pick themselves up from the ground.

"MOTHAFUCKA YOU SHOT ME . . . It's not over DL. I'm going to get you one way or another, trust that BIG BROTHER . . . I'm going to catch you when you least expect it. And that fake Bruce Lee won't be with you to save you next time" Joey said.

"MY LITTLE BROTHER Joey, trying to show me HE has some Balls, it's a little late for all that now, don't you think? So YOU took the contract? Well, let me ask you a question? Is this business or is this Personal?" DL asked.

"Its business and its personal. Remember that day at the safe house; I saw what you and Jasmine were doing in the basement that day. Do you know how that made me feel when I saw you and her having sex? She was my GIRL! You always took from me. You were dad's favorite, and I hated you for that. You were my BIG brother, I looked up to you I thought you and I were closer than that! You murdered HER! In cold blood, AND I can't let you get away with that" said Joey.

"It's not what you think Joey she had her nose in places where it shouldn't have been, she didn't love you man. She wanted what you could do for her. Once she got her degree she was going to kick you to the curb. That's what she told me, she said you were weak, and that you couldn't satisfy her. But I could . . . So now little BROTHER . . . What happened between Jasmine and I, it had nothing to do with you. But now, I know where you and I stand LITTLE BROTHA . . . So let this be a wakeup call for you, because next time, I WILL send you to your Maker" said DL.

# THE SURPRISE

Sitting in our master bathroom on the Jacuzzi were white candles in all shapes and sizes. They set the mood for romance. Hot steamy bubbles with Egyptian oils mixed with frankincense and myrrh awaited the King, and Queen. In the bedroom the same candle effect set the mood. The bed was coved with lavender, and white rose petals the scent of frankincense filled the air. Sandy was down stairs making Martinis while she waited for me to come home, Sandy had a surprise for me up stairs. Oooo wee! Then a surprise dinner was going to be at her mother's house also to celebrate my first leading role in a motion picture. I stopped off at Starbuck's again to get two more mochas because the one earlier had gotten cold. Before I went to the house I stopped off at Bernard's for him to take the mask off, I almost forgot I had it on. The little scrap I was just in with Joey and his goons left me with a bruised jaw, and a cut bottom lip now how was I going to explain that to her. I entered the house and Sandy heard the front door closing.

"Hey Baby! I'm in the kitchen!" Sandy said.

I walked into the kitchen with the two coffees I sat them down on the island. Sandy walked over to me to give me a hug and a kiss when she noticed the cut on my lip.

"You need to put something on that, the whole right side of face is swollen. Here let me get you some ice for that" Sandy said.

Sand went to the Icebox and got some cubes and put them in a plastic baggie then put it on my jaw.

I have a surprise for you sweetheart . . . What happen to you mouth baby IT'S BLEEDING" Sandy said.

"It's nothing it's just a little cut that's all. I was working out with a couple guys at the gym and I forgot to duck, I'll be fine SO . . . What's the surprise?" I replied.

"Well, it wouldn't be a surprise if I told you now would it? Let me get these drink together then you and I can go upstairs that's where the surprise is. But you have to close your eyes, and I'll lead the way" Sandy said.

Sandy walked in front of me as we went upstairs to the bedroom making sure I kept my eyes closed. When we got upstairs Sandy directed me to the bathroom. She sat our Martinis down on the Jacuzzi then took me by the hand and guided me towards her.

"Baby don't open your eyes! If you do, you will spoil the surprise! Now, walk towards me . . . Okay that's far enough hold out your arms" Sandy said.

Sandy unbuttoned and removed my shirt. She was already prepared to get in to the shower. As she loosened the belt around her housecoat, she shrugged her shoulders until the housecoat fell gracefully to the ground. Then she unbuttoned my pants, and slowly began to take them off. Past my knees one leg at a time. I stepped out of them Sandy opened the shower door, and turned on the water, the temperature was perfect. Sandy slowly stepped into the shower as I followed her she closed the door. Sandy took a shower scrub from a hook on the wall then poured some pomegranate body gel onto the palm of her hand. She started massaging me from my shoulders to my feet. When she stood up we were face to face she kissed my lips then my neck and moved to the center of my chest. As the water danced on her face as she kissed me tenderly on my chest, and then slithered herself up to my lips barely touching them as she said, "You can open your eyes now baby"

I opened my eyes kissed her on the side of her face and then on the other side. I kissed her earlobe, and each side of her neck. I turned her around and then began kissing her shoulders, down to the curve in center of her lower back near her tattoo. I picked her up slowly she wrapped her legs around my waist. I then pressed her back up against the cold tile as I kissed her collarbone, then tenderly I kissed her bottom lip. With her head arched back Sandy was in total heaven, I put her down as we remained in a tight embrace. Sandy took me by the hand and led me up, and over into the hot Jacuzzi from the shower stall. We sat down in the warm water she handed me my martini she said, "To a long life with you, sharing every moment together as we build our new empire." Sandy said

"You and I will rule the entire entertainment world together" I responded.

As we held our Martinis up gently we gave a lite toast to our successes. Sandy reached for my glass placing them both at the end of the Jacuzzi.

After setting them down she then glided over to me and ran her lips across my chest, passionately kissing my chest. It felt so good to be in her arms but I had to slow the moment down because there was something I needed to talk to her about.

"Baby, hold on I need to talk to you about something" I said.

Sandy sat up and looked at me wondering what I had to say to her. She laid her head on my chest and listened.

"Where do I even begin?" I said.

"I hope you start from the beginning" she said.

"I almost killed man because he killed a friend of mine . . . It was Jasmine I made a bad judgment call and in my anger I had Gerald and Bernard make me up to be this person Shene Hilton . . ." Jonathan Said.

"Shene? What did you do that for?" Sandy said.

"To Poison DL for what he done to Jasmine" I Said.

"Why didn't you let the police deal with that? I thought you and I went over that already?" Sandy asked.

"They were moving too slowly plus they didn't know where to find him, but I did. Bernard and Gerald made me up to look like someone he couldn't recognize. I poisoned him . . . With a green apple Martini, I spiked it with anti-freeze" I said.

"YOU DID WHAT?" Sandy asked with a shocked look on her face.

"Look let me share something with you. When I was a kid my father uses to beat the SHIT out of me. I'll never forget the look on his face when he was beating my ass. I was a little guy and to me he was this big powerful giant in my eyes. It got so bad when he would beat me I took it with a blank look on my face, determined not to cry it was as if he hated me. When I got older I told him if he ever laid another hand on me, I would kill him and I meant that. After that incident I decided to take up Martial arts. There were five of us I was the oldest out three boys and two girls, I lost my baby sister a few years ago she committed suicide. We were so frightened of that man that we all felt at peace and relief when they lowered his casket into the ground.

When DL murdered my friend Jasmine, for me it brought back horrible memories of my father. He controlled Jasmine's mind and her life just like my father controlled my life in that same fashion, it was a living HELL for all of us growing up. So I decided that I was going to get rid of him just like you get rid of trash, YOU DISPOSE OF IT" I said.

"I'm sorry you had go through that baby . . . You didn't hurt anybody did you?" Sandy said.

"Yes and no" I said.

"Jonathan what are saying? You're scaring me!" Sandy said.

"This may sound crazy but on my way home today I had a revelation. I was at Starbuck's when I met this little old lady who told me God wanted her to tell me something. She shared Isaiah 34: 8 with me from an old tattered Bible that she took from her pocket. The essence of the message was that vengeance belongs to the Lord. I cannot take His work into my own hands. I must be obedient and let Him fight my battles. The day will come when He will make all things right, and we must wait on Him" I explained.

"You are so right, Baby you didn't kill anyone right?" Sandy said.

"No I didn't kill anyone YET . . . I wasn't done telling you what happened. When the little old lady finished talking at least I thought she was, I had my head down, and when I looked up my mother was sitting across from me! Hold on, I'm not trippin'. She was really there sitting across from me! She told me to repent and go to DL ask for his forgiveness. I have a friend who practices medicine in France he can reverse the effect of the poison, but DL has to leave tomorrow he has forty eight hours to see the doctor in order to be cured," I explained

"You know what? You just had a Divine Intervention. The Lord sent an Angel to give you a message. He has given you something to do, and he wants you to concentrate on that. Let Him deal with the world and the evil people in it, it's not about you JOHNATHAN, ITS ALL ABOUT HIM. God wants you to take the talents He gave you to help others see their gifts, and to take care of your family He's got everything all under control, he don't need your help Baby!" Sandy said.

"I don't want God to ever turn His back on me and take my blessings away from us. I Love the Lord, and I would never do anything to lose favor with Him. That's why I had to make amends with DL I'm a Christian, and I am my brother's keeper" I explained.

"You're a beautiful man and I am so glad God put us together. I am proud to be Mrs. Jonathan Paul. He's going to always see us through if we keep Him first in our lives. We can't do anything without Him TRUELY this is not about us Baby, it's all about God but you know what? Sandy said.

"Tell me Baby, cause I know you're gonna tell me anyway," I replied.

"We're going to be alright we just have to keep it pushin'. What are you going to do about DL?" Sandy asked.

"He's going to meet me and Boy's at the studio tomorrow night. We're going to give him another Identity, and help him get out of the country. He's not liked by a lot of people right about now that's why I have to do it this way," I explained.

"Okay you do what you think is right baby. I think it's time to get out of this tub, I'm starting to look like a prune you know something? I Love you so much it hurts. If you stick with Jesus you got me for life," Sandy said.

Sandy and I got out of the Jacuzzi and dried ourselves off. As we entered the bedroom, I took one look at the bed, and one look at Sandy.

"No my brotha. That's part of the surprise that will come later on tonight so back up! Put your tongue back in your mouth Babe, but you know what? It meant a lot to me to hear you tell me what's going on with you," Sandy said to me.

"You're my wife I can't hide anything from you, I want you to always trust me because I love you." I told her.

"And I love you more . . . Babie I want you to do something for me. I know we don't have much time, and I don't want us to be late to our dinner engagement, but can you sing to me?" She replied.

"What do you want me to sing for you sweetheart? Jonathan said.

"That song you wrote for our wedding "Love Me" I didn't know you could sing like. That's the song you have as your ringtone on your phone" Sandy said.

"There's a lot still you don't know about me, but it's all good because it's gonna take a life time to share it all with you." Jonathan said.

"I don't have a problem with that." Sandy replied.

# THE GAME PLAN

My beautiful wife and I pulled up in front of her parent's home. We arrived at the front gate I rolled down the window on the driver side reached my out my arm and pushed the button on the intercom. The gate swung open and we drove down a cobbled stone driveway that led to a gorgeous colorful flowered courtyard.

I parked the car and we walked through the court that led to the front door. Sandy opened the door and walks through the foyer straight into her parent's kitchen. The kitchen floor was covered with natural tile, Black marble counter tops rested along the walls. Near the center of the kitchen sat a Sushi Island with a built in cooking range.

All the cabinetry in the kitchen was made of red oak wood with glass door facings trimmed in gold leaf, and to the right stood black stainless steel doubled stack oven that was built into the wall. Across from the oven were a walk in refrigerator, and a walk in pantry next to it. Across from the Sushi Island was a doubled stainless steel sink. I followed Sandy's voice down into my new in-laws den. On the west wall was a 100" flat screen TV built into the wall along with the sound system. It was like being in a theater it had a large fireplace that sat next to the flat screen. I could see An Olympic size pool lit up in the backyard ready for anyone's enjoyment. In the floor in the middle of the den the pool began and then led out into the backyard. A drinking bar ran all along the kitchen wall, it was a very elegant place. Sandy's mother was the bartender for the night looks like Peter was feeling pretty good my father-In-Law was very emotionally intoxicated.

"There's my son-in-law!! Come on down and have a seat! What's your poison? Connie is the bartender for the night I have to say, she's doing a pretty good job. What are you drinking Joa . . . Joan . . . . Nath . . . ?" said Peter.

"Daddy! Daddy!" Sandy said.

"What Baby? Come here I want to tell you something, Come here," Peter said.

Sandy walked over to her father he pulled her close to him and then grabbed me by the wrist then pulled us both in close, like a group hug.

"Daddy we can hear you! You don't have to talk so loud!" Sandy said.

Peter brought his tone down to bond with his children.

"Ok, Ok . . . You've made your mother, and I so proud. You're my firstborn I longed for the day to see you walk down that aisle YOU WERE SO BEAUTIFUL . . . My little girl is all grown up and married now. You're a good man JOHNATHAN. I know you will take good care of my little girl, I KNOW that you really LOVE MY LITTLE GIRL, Who knows one day you, may have to run Supreme studios just like me, ONLY BETTER. I've heard things around the lot about your new venture with Bernard and Gerald, What's it called? HLLS? What is that?" Peter said.

"Well Dad, HLLS are acronyms for Human Life—Like—Skin," I said.

"He's well-spoken too! Did you go to college?" Peter asked.

"Yes sir I did, I went to Drewman," I replied.

"Did you now? I knew I liked you from the start! "OPN" Omega Phi Nu . . . FO, Life . . . My brother and I went there too what was you major?" Peter asked.

"Computer Technology, I took it a step further and studied to be a computer technician in robotics" I said.

"Let me ask you something when are you two going to start filling my back yard up with little geniuses like their father? I want to let you know something you're creative ideas are going to make you guy's very wealthy men very soon. Think about what it will do for the movie business smart Stocks and bonds all the way! Before you know it HLLS will blow sky high" Peter said.

The doorbell rang and the house butler answered the door. It was Michael with his secretary, as they walked in the butler took their coats then hung them up in the guest bedroom. Michael and his secretary walked through the kitchen and into the den to join the rest of the family.

"Speaking of the DEVIL! There he is! Michael, come, come sit here next to you big brother, we have a lot to talk about tonight. You my son-in-law and I are going to make a lot of money . . . I got a call from Mattel today they want to start manufacturing action hero dolls in the likeness of Jonathan. Also Gatorade contacted me and informed me that they intend to start a campaign to promote 'JP Quick Energy Drink'. Personally I would like for those two projects to be out on the market before the movie hits the box office, what are you drinking?" Peter said.

"What are you drinking Jonathan? That looks pretty good" Michael said.

"Green apple martini," Jonathan replied.

"Connie, fix me one of those! So what's the game plan?" Michael asked

"One green apple martini coming up . . . What time is Jonathan's call time for tomorrow? I think it's been changed from night shoots to day shoots due to something about permits not being ready. That's why we're going to shoot all the love scenes between Jonathan and Vivaca first; we'll be shooting on stage seven. Tammy what time is Vivaca supposed to be on set tomorrow?" Connie said.

Tammy searched her Blackberry referring to her notes.

"I have her down for eight with Jonathan. Two night's shoots for the car chase, and three nights for the club scene in downtown LA and three nights for the hospital scene" Tammy said.

"Will six of those nights be shot on the lot?" Michael asked.

"Yea we are going have to switch slots with Teen Vampire. They're going to use stage twelve, and we are going to use stage seven. Have the stage crew start building the set for the hospital tomorrow. How many days do you think we need to shoot all the love scenes?" Connie inquired.

"If Vivaca can remember all her lines we could wrap it up in five days, and then move on to the hospital scenes" Peter answered.

"Okay, that sound's good. Tammy could you please call her right now, and tell her that the shooting schedule has been changed. Starting tomorrow we're going to start shooting her love scenes with Jonathan. Tell her to be on the set at 10:00 am tomorrow morning on stage seven" Connie said.

Suddenly the sound of the dinner bell rang summoning us to the table.

"Dinner is ready to be served in the dinning area," announced the butler. "Come this way please" he said politely.

The dinner table was set with fine silverware and china. A female kitchen servant filled the water glasses and placed them around the table as the family members took their seats. Peter and I sat at opposite ends of the dinner table. Sandy and her mother sat across from one other. Tammy was seated to the right of Connie and Michael was seated to the right of Sandy. Another servant brought hot dinner rolls to the table as another placed our salads in front of us.

"Jonathan will you bless the food?" Peter asked.

The room became silent the servants and the butler stood at attention with their heads bowed in preparation for the prayer.

"Our Most Gracious Heavenly Father the eyes of all look to You O Lord you give us food at the proper time. You open Your Hand and satisfy the desires of every living thing. Father, bless the hands that prepared this meal. Bless us oh Lord and these Thy gifts which we all here are about to receive from Your Bountiful Goodness all these things we ask to be done through Your Son Jesus Christ, our Lord and Savior everyone say Amen" Jonathan prayed.

"Amen. Amen and Amen," the family said in unison.

"Well, let's eat! Okay Michael here's the game plan there was Elvis, and then there was Bruce Lee those two guys made lot of money for the studios they were signed with. My son-in-law is both of those actors all in one. He can sing, fight, do all of his own stunts, write and direct. Oooo and Connie let the camera director and the stunt coordinator know now, that Jonathan will coordinate and direct his own fight scenes you got that? Make a note of that Tammy" Peter ordered.

"It's done we never finished with everybody's call time Vivaca's is at ten in the morning if she has to be on set at that time I think Jonathan should be there also. They can rehearse with the director then by the time they get to hair and makeup it'll be eleven o'clock we'll break for lunch. Ok, so that means we'll start shooting around 2:00 in the afternoon" Tammy said.

"Ok, we will get our eight hours in, and if everything goes well we should be wrapped around ten o'clock at night. If we don't run into any technical problems we can be done with both of them in a few days" Connie said.

"I can live with that, Jonathan is there anything you would like to say regarding what we were talking about? I'm making you co-producers on this project, so feel free to jump in at anytime with any ideas you have to make this project better." Peter said.

"Okay Dad" Jonathan replied.

"HE CALLED ME DAD! He called me Dad! Connie! He called me Dad" Peter said with excitement.

"I hear you Baby! Sandy, don't let your father drink anymore tonight. He started after the pool man left around eleven o'clock this morning, now that just ridiculous don't you think so?" Connie said.

"You were the one fixing the drinks and giving them to him before we got here! Maybe when he finishes eating he'll sit down somewhere, and go to sleep" Sandy said.

At the end of the first course the kitchen help removed our salad plates. Now the main course featured honey-baked turkey with mushrooms and white gravy poured over a tasty well-seasoned dressing with mashed potatoes were being placed on the table. Along with platters of cabbage warm golden brown corn bread dripping with hot butter, my goodness, almost before my plate settled on the table it was almost gone. Dinner with the In-laws was a hit. I hadn't had meal like that since I left Texas Connie knows what she's doing in the kitchen. Not long after the main course was served my favorite dessert chocolate mousse was presented at the table. Sandy told her mother that she and I had the same culinary taste, and this was the surprise that Sandy had referred to earlier.

Suddenly I received a call from my old college friend Doctor Kajai Ferrell he was a "Toxicologist" in "Toxicology" dealing with the effects, Antidotes, detection etc of Poisons he was from India. Dr. Ferrell bears resemblance to Jerry Bruckheimer. He was returning my call regarding DL's illness so I excused myself from the table to take the call. I left the dining room and retreated to Connie's garden room near the foyer.

"Oh my God! Jonathan Paul! How have you been man?" Kajai said.

"I'm good Kajai what about yourself?" I said.

"I can't complain life is good to me! I just opened a clinic in Paris about a year ago. I've been blessed to help the unfortunate. We help people who can't afford medical help it's a tax write-off for me, and it's my way of giving back to society you know. What can I do for you my friend?" Kajai said.

"It's a long story someone I know is very sick they ingested some antifreeze about three days ago, it was kind of my fault. I remembered this was your area of expertise, so that's why I called you to see if you could help me" I said.

"Same old Jonathan . . . You still have that temper Hun? How much did he ingest?" Kajai asked.

"About eight grams" I replied.

"Oh my God, how much would say he weighs?" Kajai continued.

"I'd say about 205 . . . 215, somewhere around there" I said.

"If he doesn't get to a doctor within forty eight hours he will die for sure. The antifreeze will burn his esophagus and his intestines then his kidney will shut down. There will be a lot of sweating coughing and severe vomiting Wow, this guy is really messed up! Be sure you tell him to drink lots of milk; in the meantime he needs to come see me ASAP he's running out of time. If he is starting to spit up a lot of blood it won't be long before death will take him, every second is important. My address is 227 Padre Road. Call me when you get to the airport, I'll meet the two of you at my clinic. Hurry Jonathan, time is of the essence you must move without delay" Kajai said.

OK we'll be on the first available flight to Paris tonight. Thanks Kajai we'll see you soon" I said.

I hung up the phone and returned to the dining room Sandy noticed that something was wrong when I sat down.

"Baby is everything all right? You look worried about something?" Sandy inquired.

"I'll talk to you about it later sweetheart we need to leave now something's come up" I told her in a calm voice.

"Hey Jonathan my brother and I are going to step out in the back yard for a smoke. I have some more Cuban cigars; these babies were dipped in cognac this time would you want to join us?" Peter asked.

"Look, I would love to but something has come up Sandy and I need to leave, Connie the food was off the hook I really enjoyed myself tonight. Did we address all of the business matters we needed to discuss?" I said.

"Yes we covered everything that we needed to talk about we're good" Peter said.

"I have three check here for you from lumbar Pictures" Michael said.

The checks all totaled to seventy five thousand dollars. Lumbar Pictures sent the checks last week but Michael was just now getting around to giving them to me. Michael handed the checks to Sandy to give to me she glanced at them then quickly folded them and put them in her bra.

"I'll take that . . . Mom I'll call you later dinner was great. I guess we'll see everyone bright and early tomorrow morning" Sandy said cheerfully.

"Yes you will sweetheart . . . Come and give your father a big hug before you leave" Peter said.

Sandy got up from the table and gave him a big hug and a kiss on the cheek. Everyone got up from the table then walked Sandy and I to the front door I hugged Connie and then shook Peters hand before we left.

"Sandy I need to leave for Paris tonight with DL. My old college friend Kajai Ferrell is a doctor in Paris, I told him about DL he said he could help him. He's "Toxicologist" he said it's important that he sees DL within forty-eight hours if he doesn't, DL will surely die. I just can't have his blood on my hands I need God to continue to bless this family I need to do all I can to help this man it's my entire fault that he's in this condition" I confided in Sandy.

"Don't beat yourself up about it it's going to all work itself out. Just do your part and give the rest to God he will work it all out for you" Sandy said.

"There's more to that story I need to help him get out of the country because there are others who want DL dead" I said.

"All of this is due to what happened to Jasmine right? You were trying to avenge her death and you thought you were doing the right thing, little did you know that you were about to cut off your blessings. Do you really think it was a smart thing for you to get involved with DL and all his mess?" Sandy asked.

"No it wasn't smart . . . I needed to undo what I did by getting medical help for him. DL is suppose to meet me at the studio later on tonight. Gerald and Bernard are going to give him a face lift and a new identity so he can get out of the country" I said.

Sandy reached for my hand and then held it tight. She began to cry so I pulled to the side of the road to take her in my arms, and console her.

"Baby everything is going to be all right! Why are you crying?" I asked.

"I asked God to send me a good Godly man, and he did. I don't want to lose you behind some foolishness. I just want everything to go back the way it was. I want you to continue making films become a big star in Hollywood and together we can raise our children in our beautiful home. I want that so bad baby; I just don't want anything to happen to you!" Sandy said tearfully.

"I'm going to be just fine we'll have more children then you and I will grow old together, and see our grand children grow up in this big beautiful home. I love you Sandy, I would not do anything to jeopardize what God has blessed me with. I have a sweet beautiful kind-hearted wife, and you know what, you are my gift from God" I told her lovingly.

"I needed to hear that from you" Sandy said.

I leaned over and kissed her tenderly on the lips. I wanted her to understand that everything was under control, and that she is the most important thing in my life. Sandy means the world to me and we were going to get through this together.

"Take me home then go handle your business when you're done I'll be waiting for you and I'll have another surprise for you" she told me.

"There's more? I hate when you do that! Now you're going to leave me hanging wondering about that surprise" I said.

"Don't you think life would be boring if we always knew the outcome of everything? A little mystery makes life interesting. Haven't you ever seen two elderly people sitting on a park bench holding hands and smiling at one another like high school sweet hearts?" Sandy asked.

"Yes I've seen that many times what's your point?" I inquired.

"They share their love by giving each other little surprises. If they're Christians they understand that the secret of staying together is keeping God first in their lives. That is our game plan too Jonathan we're going to be those two elderly people someday" Sandy said.

"I couldn't agree with you any more than that, that's a great game plan," I said.

I pulled up into our driveway drove through the gates and then stopped in front of the front door. I gave Sandy a kiss on the lips to reassure her that everything was going to be all right and that I would be back as soon as DL had gotten away safely. Sandy got out of the car then walked to the top of the steps. Like a little kid she watched me, as I backed out of the drive way, then drove off down the street.

# THE ESCAPE

D L and I pull up to the side entrance of the supreme studios lot on Gower with DL sitting on the passenger side. The guard raised the gate and I drove onto the lot, and parked next to my office in front of stage 11. We got out of the SUV walked over to my office I open the door looked around to see if anyone was watching. I motioned for DL to come inside once inside I locked the door behind me we walked down a small hallway and entered the room where Bernard and Gerald were waiting to give DL his new Identity.

There was not much time to waste so I directed DL to sit in the makeup chair. Bernard and Gerald began to do their magic Gerald cleaned DL's face with hydrogen peroxide then next he took some HLLS with a small brush, and then covered DL's entire face so they could get a smooth texture. DL had sores on his face and Bernard wanted that natural look as if nothing were wrong with his face.

As Barnard finished mixing the plaster for DL's face Bernard inserted two straws in his nose then smoothed plaster all over his head and face. Soon the mold was ready in no time it was off. Bernard lightly pulled the molds off and then placed them on a workbench. Gerald poured the HLLS into the molds it didn't take long before it was ready. He pulled the latex from the mold and started cutting out pieces to place on DL's face then the magic began. DL was being transformed Bernard placed each piece gently on to his face as he tried not to cause him any more pain than he has dealt with already. Bernard put on DL's eye brows and touched up the nose with some special make up for binding all of the pieces together to look like one mass of skin. Gerald applied the hair cap by putting glue on the inside of it and placed it on DL's head. Small dabs of glue was placed around the hairline to make it blend in with the latex, it gave him a completed and convincing look. Bernard handed DL a mirror then stepped back Gerald and Jonathan waited in anticipation for DL's approval. DL ran his fingers lightly across his face then looked at both sides of it. He played with his hair checking out the new look.

"Ya'll good . . . I see why the two of you are in such high demand in this business. It's unbelievable what the two of you can do to somebody's face" I said.

DL looked like a combination of Paul McCartney and Richard Gear. I looked at my watch it was 10:00 p.m. DL got up from the chair when Bernard told me to hold on.

"Jonathan before you leave I want to show you something. I'm sure you're gonna LOVE this Ninja" Bernard said.

Bernard opened the door to a room and everyone follows him. We all walked in "I can't see anything! What's up with the lights Dog" I said.

Bernard turns on the lights and in the center of the room sat the Black Cobra. I couldn't believe my eyes.

"O-my-God! When did you restore it?" I said.

I walked along the side of the car touching it like a kid on Christmas day. Gerald opened the door I took a seat behind the wheel and started the engine. The dash looked like the cockpit of a fighter plane the entire set up was digital. It had a brand new state of the art 512 gig computer with a 5G network with voice command and satellite GPS on star tracking system on board.

"Don't the two of you have somewhere to be? I think you need to go take care of your business like right now . . . and be safe my brother" Bernard said.

DL got into the Cobra on the passenger side and closed the door then put on his seat belt. Bernard pushed a button on the wall next to where he was standing the garage door rolled up. I put the car in drive then hit the gas petal burning rubber out of the sound stage headed for LAX. We hit Melrose going eastbound as we approached Western Avenue the light turned red we come to a complete stop. In the lane to my left Joey was making a left turn he looked over at me and recognized who I was. The light turned green I took off as Joey followed close behind me.

"Look! Is that the guy we ran into at the Club the other night?" Joey said.

"Yea . . . That's him who is that in the car with him?" the Gangster said.

"Some white boy I ain't worried about him I want the driver. That's who I want" Joey said.

I looked in my rear view mirror and saw Joey tailing behind me. I approached the on ramp to the 101 the light was red so I came to a full stop then waited for the red light to turn green. Still looking in my rear view mirror I turned on the computers LCD screen. It allowed me see the car license plates behind me through a rear view backup camera GPS monitor with the latest Tom Tom navigation system on board. I could see who was driving in the car behind me real good.

"DL . . . Look at the screen; does that person look familiar to you?" I said.

"That's Joey . . . What's your plan?" DL said.

"I'm going to have some fun with him hold on" I said.

The light turned green I floor it. As we made a sharp right turn on to the freeway Joey was right behind me. We were flying down the freeway weaving in and out of traffic each car we passed it look like they were standing still. I got into the merging lane for the Harbor Freeway south. I started breaking it down speed shifting to slow this monster down once out of the curve I popped the clutch twice and my tiers screamed as we ripped down the highway. Joey was trying his best to keep up with me without wrecking his car we were long gone. We got to the Manchester off ramp I started to slow it down then pulled over, and turn off my lights. Joey was flying he shot right past us he was so focused on catching up that he didn't see my car parked on the shoulder of the freeway.

"What are you doing?" DL said.

"The escapes of the century just relax and enjoy the ride . . ." I said.

I turn on my lights revved up the engine and merged into the traffic I took off running to catch up with Joey. The 105 westbound was coming up soon I couldn't see Joey ahead of me. As Joey made the turn merging onto the 105 I pull up alongside of him revving my engine. I look over at Joey smiled at him then took off Joey was right behind me trying to keep up.

"Watch this" I said.

I slowed down again we were coming up to the Crenshaw exit Joey was right on my bumper. I pushed a button on the console a camera emerged I took a picture of Joey's license plate. I then moved to the right of Joeys SUV slowed down got behind the SUV Joey keep going. I typed in some information on the Computer System then entered a secret code that would shut down the engine to Joey's car.

"All systems down on 2010 Lincoln SUV . . ." the On Star system voice announced.

Joey's car slowed down to a complete stop.

"What the? This car is brand new this can't be happing! Look! They are getting away" Joey said.

Joey's SUV was parked on the shoulder of the freeway we flew right past them blowing the horn. We approached the on ramp to the 405 north and then exited Century East to LAX.

"This car looks familiar" DL said.

"Does it now? That's funny you would say that. A friend of mine died in this car yesterday he was hit on the driver's side, and pushed off the side of a cliff on Mulholland. What do you know about that?" I said.

"This car we are riding in right now! Yeah I did that he had it coming to him" D.L said.

"Is that right? Don't believe everything you see or hear in Hollywood because a lot of time it's not what it appears to be. Looks like you got punked, it was all staged Doog" I said.

"Yeah it's time for me to get out of the exterminating business and get a life I'm really getting to old for this shit here" DL said.

"Yeah . . . I know what you mean. But first you need to get your life right, then you can look forward to that dream of getting your life back in order you know what I mean" I said.

"I know what you mean . . . I hear you loud and clear" DL replied.

I pulled into the L.A.X parking lot across from where we had to go. We got out of the car and rushed over to American Airlines to board the flight for Paris that was leaving in ten minuets. DL and I walked into the terminal since DL had no luggage so it made it easy for him to get right on the plane. I stopped in my tracks to let D.L know he has to go by himself. I reached into my pocket and took out a folded piece of paper with Doctor Kajai Ferrell information on it; I put it in his hands.

"Hey! Look DL I'm not going with you, I don't even want know where you're going. I think it will better that way for you and me everything you need to know is on that paper I just gave you. Kajai will help you get well he's a very good friend of mine" I said.

"I'm goanna ask you again why are you doing this? You could have not told me anything and just let me die. For all the wrong I've done, that would have been the price I just would have had to pay. I know what time it is . . . that's part of the game Dog" DL said.

"D.L two wrongs don't make a right. I had to make a change in my life too; you see Part of me was just like you. I know the difference between right and wrong, I was taught that from a kid and now I'm a Christen man. It's not right, see I created Shene to do all the bad things I wouldn't do but it would have caught up with me eventually. Now that part of me is dead and gone I've been blessed . . . Everybody deserves a second chance in life to get back on track look at it like this: God works miracles you ingested a deadly dose of antifreeze through a drink, you're not suppose be here, you catch my drift?" I said.

"Drift caught, good lookin . . ." DL said.

"Flight 707 leaving for Paris now boarding . . . Flight 707 leaving for Paris now boarding . . . Thank you for flying American Airlines" the announcement blared over the intercom.

Just then DL saw Joey with seven other guys at the end of the terminal walking their way.

"At six o'clock Joey and his crew are walking this way" DL said softly.

I turned to see how close Joey was I ducked behind the escalator and slide on my belly to the other side then up to the second level as DL made his escape. Joey caught a glimpse of me up stairs they all ran to catch me. I backed myself up into a wall and got into a strong on guard stance. As they got closer I could see the fear in there eyes. With them just a few feet in front of me with a quick side step and shuffle I lunged a sidekick and planted my foot right in this guy's chest that sent him flying into two other goons knocking them down like bowling pins.

Like a cat I slowly made my way towards the escalator. Another guy attacked me from behind, and without even looking at him I turned with a wild down ward swing, with my left fist, hitting him square on the side of his face. Then with my right fist I exploded with a right upper cut to his jaw knocking him smooth out. I continued to walk down stairs when two other guys attacked me from each side. I dropped to one knee punching with my left fist to one guys' groin he fell to the ground, I hit the other guy with a open palm strike to his face breaking his nose slowly I turned then shoved the guy down the escalator backwards. I continued walking past him ready to destroy anything that got in my way.

Joey didn't have any more back up just one guy left; he remembered the beating I gave him in our last encounter he was not about to get in my way. I stopped and looked at Joey with a hard stair. As I held my head down hardly even looking at him I began to ball up my fist, as I prepared myself in a strong fighting stance like a pit bull ready to destroy anything that crossed my path. Joey stopped in his tracks.

"My beef is not with you this is between DL and myself it's a family matter . . . Just business nothing personal, WERE DONE HERE!" Joey said.

In slow motion Joey motioned to the rest of his goons to leave with him. They were out classed since they had to leave their guns outside in the car due to tight security at LAX. Without their heat they were nothing. If this rumble would have happened anywhere else it would have been a body count for sure.

Flight 707 was slowly rolling down the runway it began its ascent into the sky soon it would be out of sight in route to Paris France.

A black limo is cruising down a dark road it slowed down then stopped in front of a mansion. Seven men got out of the limo and walked through a gated courtyard toward the mansion. Men in dark suites stood in different areas of the mansion with automatic weapons in their hands. The seven men walked up some flight of stairs to a room with a large table; sitting at the head of a table was the dark figure of a man smoking a cigar. The room looked like a library with books all along the walls a large conference table sat in the center of the room. The seven men all took a seat at the table.

"You're here with good news to give me I take it?" the dark figure said.

"Well not exactly" Joey said.

"What do you mean 'not exactly'? Do you think this is a game we're playing?" the man said.

"No sir" Joey said.

The dark figure motioned his hand to one of the guards to come to the table. He held out his hand the guard gave him a gun the dark figure laid the gun down on the table, and continued talking.

"You said you wanted to take care of that matter what happened?" said the man with the cigar.

"I don't have an answer, give me another chance to hit him I just need a little more time" Joey said.

The man seated at the table picked up the gun and pointed it at Joey's head.

"Give you more TIME I can't do that son, I knew I couldn't depend on you to get the job done. You're week you've always been a fuck up your entire life, you have given this family nothing but Problem. And you want me to give you more time? I can't do that Joey time is money. This is a business son you have become a liability to me, and you let me down, this is for your own good. You're just in the world in the way, Joey . . . Tell your mother hello for me" said the man with the cigar.

He pulled the trigger. POW! Joey's brains splattered all over the bookshelves behind him in slow motion Joey slumped down into his chair and flopped on top of the table like a pancake. Blood and brain matter splattered everywhere.

"I HATE THAT! If you want something done you have to do it yourself. Take this garbage away and clean up this mess the rest of you boys let this be a lesson for you, in this game you never bite off more than you can chew because your word is bond. Donte' take these gentlemen downstairs and pay them for their services" said the man.

Donte' escorted the remaining six men out of the room down stairs when Gunshots from a semi automatic broke the silence. The man swung his chair around and faced a picture of a man sitting in a big black leather chair with an owl on the back of his chair perched over his left shoulder. He had salt and pepper hair and wore a white suite with the likeness of Scar Face hanging on the wall. The figure stood up and walked over to the picture to readjust its position on the wall the man in the picture was Joey and DL's father Larry B. Love.

Joey and DL were brothers they had the same father but different mothers. At thirty years of age DL was the oldest Joey was just 27 years old since childhood Joey always tried to impress his father, wanting to show him he was the better son and could be the most responsible out of the two. There was nothing he wouldn't do to have his father's favor DL was more like his father than Joey. DL was ruthless and cold—hearted he was the perfect son. His father loved him more than Joey because he was in love with DL's mother she gave him his first born, so he would spend more time showing DL the ropes.

Joey's mother was a hooker and a drug addict. She died while giving birth to him. Joey's selfish and overconfident ways led him to his demise by the man who gave him life. DL's father had a plan it was to build a close bloodline of killers that were just like him. He wanted people that he could trust that would have his back unconditionally. It was a family of coldhearted ruthless killers that he wanted to create. It was all about trying to get the almighty dollar and calling all the shots in that dark world of human extermination.

Larry always had a back up to his game plan there was always a method to his madness. He had two other sons and one daughter by three different mothers, Butch Love who was 24 years old with a great build and a bad behavior problem. He had olive color skin green eyes and always kept his hair cut neatly. He held three world champion titles in marksmanship. Then there was Tony Love a male thinly built he was 23 year-old with red caramel colored skin, very high strung with a pit bull type mentality he could be as cool as he wanted to be but it wasn't wise to cross him.

Samaria Love, Larry's heart she was a cute 20 years old with a round face pretty deep blue eyes that could sweep you off your feet. She had a caramel tone to her skin and high cheekbones always wearing the newest hairstyle to complete her beautiful personality. She could instantly turn deadly with her charming cunning ways. They all waited in the wings to get their first assignment from their father to carry out his orders by any means necessary they all compete against one another to be next one in line to run the family business.

# CHECKING THE GATE

It was 9:45 Thursday morning I was rolling in my limo on my way to Supreme studios it was the first day of shooting of Hunters Revenge. I arrived on the set as the limo parked in front of my trailer the studio had provided bodyguards for me throughout the show. The driver opened the door I stepped out of the limo, and their standing beside the door was a bodyguard.

"How you doing my brother? Jonathan Paul" I said.

"It's nice to meet you Mr. Paul. My name is Trey Adams I'm at your service, if you need anything just halla at me" Trey said.

Trey was a large Afro American male who was built like a soldier. He was clean cut wore a black double-breasted suite a black bow tie and a pair of black Stacy Adams to complement his look.

"You got it Trey I'll be talking to you, I need to get in this trailer and see what they have crackin' for me . . . I like those shoes my man!" I said.

"You like these? Alright then, I have a hook up through a friend of mine. I got you my brotha what size shoe you wear?" Trey said.

"Eleven I want some just like those you're wearing right there" I said.

"Okay you got that you have a nice day Mr. Paul!" Trey said.

I entered my trailer wardrobe had prepared three changes of clothes in my closet for each of the scenes to be shot this morning. I took a seat on the couch and next to where I was sitting on a table were my sides for today's shooting. I had three scenes to shoot with Vivaca It was going to be a very interesting day. Vivaca was in makeup and her day was not starting out right. Vivaca's assistant brought her a hot cup of coffee and as she handed it to Vivaca she spilled it all over her wardrobe the dress was ruined and the steaming coffee burned her wrist.

"Oh! Shit girl! What the hell's wrong with you? Look what you've done! Now wardrobe has to find me something else to wear. It was hard enough trying finding this outfit! Go! Go! You're done! Go let wardrobe know what happened and when you're done take the rest of the day off!" Vivaca said.

"Vivaca! Don't be so hard on her! This is her first job ever! The girl is nervous she didn't mean to spill the coffee on you. Accidents do happen, Baby look don't pay her any mind go and tell wardrobe to send somebody over here with a change of clothes for Vivaca," The makeup artist said.

"Do I still have to go home Miss Poxin? I really need this job!" The assistant said.

"No you don't have to go home just pay attention to what you're doing girl! I'm sorry for yelling at you my bad" Vivaca said.

The assistant left the trailer as she left the first AD came to the door.

"We're going to need you on set in thirty minutes when you're done here I'll come and get you and take you to the set" the AD said.

"I'm having a change of wardrobe sent to my trailer I spilled coffee all over what I'm wearing now. When they make the change I'll be ready. Why don't you call them and see what's up with my cloths" Vivaca said.

The AD got on her walkie-talkie to find out what was going on with Vivaca's change of clothes.

"I need someone to go over to wardrobe and get a change of clothes for Vivaca. She spilled coffee all over her clothes . . . All right thanks. They just sent someone to your trailer with a new outfit for you. I'll see you shortly" The AD said.

Sandy and her mother were walking up to my trailer as they arrived at the door Trey opens it for them they entered the trailer and Sandy had another surprise for me. It was tucked away in her purse.

"Hey Baby! How are you doing? Are you nervous yet?" Sandy asked.

"A little bit, and that too shall soon pass. It's funny when I was in Jr. High I was the laughing stock of Whaley Jr. High school if they could only see me now" I said.

"Peter has big plans for you Jonathan He's going to make you a big Star you have no idea what Supreme has in store for you you're just getting started" Connie said.

Just then a puppy started whimpering I looked around to see where the sound was coming from.

"That sounds like . . . It's a puppy! Where is it?" said.

Sandy opened her purse and took out a puppy then handed it to me I was so happy this was a good surprise.

"Wow! This is so cool I've always wanted a blue pit this way cool Man. aw and you brought my suit for tomorrow Thanks Baby . . ." I said.

I took a moment to reflect on the reason I was going to Shene's funeral it was closure for me. Shene's death represented my alter ego that dark side of me. I created someone to do my dirty work for me now I'm rid of that Demon and he will rest he no longer lives inside of me, I'm a changed man It was time for me to move forward and do the right things in life.

"Baby what's wrong? Are you alright?" Sandy said.

"I'm fine I was just thinking about Shene, he was a very close friend of mine that had some really bad ways about him but overall he was a good guy he was alright . . . just a little misunderstood I'm going to miss the old boy" I said.

Sandy walked over to where I was sitting and hugged me and the puppy Connie sat down at the table slid my plate of food in front of her and removed the cover it was a breakfast burger with hash browns.

"Why are you letting this food go to waste? If you don't want it I'll eat it" Connie said.

"Go ahead mom I'll get something to eat later I'm not really that hungry," I said.

There was a knock at the door It was the AD she had come to take me to the set Sandy opened the door.

"Okay Jonathan they're ready for you on set I'm going to walk you over . . . Oh! Lookie! A puppy! He's so cute! Can I hold him?" the AD said.

"It's a female" Sandy said.

"Sure you can hold her" I said.

I handed the puppy to the AD. She took the puppy in her arms and hugged and kissed her on the head.

"I'm sorry, can I take care of her while you're shooting?" the AD pleaded.

"Well my wife . . ." I began to say.

"That's your puppy I don't have anything to do with that. Mother and I are going shopping and you have to work dear I just stopped by to bring you DOG" Sandy said.

Connie Sandy and I left for the set. Trey walked with us to the set another and his brother from his crew walked along side us in the front with the AD and Trey following behind.

"Dog? That's what she is, she needs a real name something like Treyah or Herculea" I said.

"That's her name D-O-G baby? But you can change it if you like she's your dog" Sandy said.

We got to the set and I sat in my chair next to the director's chair. Other workers saw the AD with the puppy they all wanted to hold her.

Okay baby, mama and I are out here we'll be back later break a leg" Sandy said.

As Sandy and her mother were leaving they heard all this noise outside the sound stage. It sounded like two women arguing it was "Hey! Hey! What's going on out here? Vivaca what's the problem?" Connie said.

"Good morning Connie this morning I had some coffee spilled on my cloths wardrobe didn't answer my calls so I went to them. I went to MY rack where MY entire wardrobe is kept I started looking through them and I found this! She tried to stop me. So I pushed her out of the way and got my clothes then she followed me all the way over her telling me what I can and cannot do. Does she even know who I am?" Vivaca said.

"Okay everybody slow your roll, this is the first day of shooting for everybody. There's going to be a lot of new faces on this set. We all need to just get along we can't do this. This is not professional ladies we're not going to conduct ourselves in this manner, do I make myself clear? Debbie, this is Vivaca Poxin, one of the studios stars if she needs you to get something get it for her and whatever she wants LET HER HAVE IT. Do you understand?" Connie said.

"Yes ma'am I understand . . ." Debbie said.

Debbie walked back to the wardrobe trailer she was a small frame Jewish girl with black spiked hair and tattoos on her arms. She wore black lipstick and yellow contact lenses in her eyes. She had a mysterious vampire look. She had a straightforward personality dressed with a grunge fashion Goth like look. Vivaca and Connie were still talking when the AD walked over to where Sandy Connie and Vivaca were standing.

"Excuse me Connie but they need Vivaca on set right now" the AD announced.

"Okay, you go on and do your thing. My daughter and I were on our way out I'll talk to later Vivaca. AND BE NICE!" Connie said.

I was already on set talking to the director about the scene and what he wanted to capture on film.

"Okay Jonathan what's going on with Kim and Paris is this; Paris is a Bounty Hunter he is about to pick up a very dangerous killer and take her to jail her name is Kim White. Before he turns her over to the police they have some unfinished business to take care of" the director said.

Just then Vivaca walked on to the set then over to her chair as she takes her seat, she began to stare at Jonathan with lust in her eyes.

"That's Peter's new son in-law look like somebody's gotten your attention, don't even think about it if you do you'll never work again in Hollywood sista" the assistant said" Let me ask you a question? What would you be willing to sacrifice to live the good life? Asked the assistant.

"Almost anything . . . if I can't get what I want one way, I'll get it another way . . . no matter what gets in my way I will have what I WANT take notes chick" Vivaca said.

Vivaca got up from her seat and switched over to where Jonathan and the director were standing then glared back at the assistant.

"Hello Vivaca I was just explaining to Jonathan what was going on with Kim and Paris you wanna get started" the director said.

The director walked towards the camera the assistant cameraman took a measuring tape hooked it to the front of the camera and walks towards the bed. Vivaca and I stood together talking while the crew was setting up for the first shot.

"I hear you just got married" Vivaca said.

"Yes, I did it was this past Saturday" I replied.

"I know her dad spent a lot of money on your wedding whatever baby girl wants is what baby girl gets. You two make a great couple, Well let's get ready to do this It's going to be fun working with you" Vivaca said.

"The first shot will be of Paris taking hand cuffs off Kim's wrist. Then they will begin to hug and kiss Paris will lead Kim to the bed and that will be the end of the scene . . . OK let's go for picture" the director said.

"Okay, this is a closed set now if you're not the talent and you're not in this shot you need to leave now. Okay people, looks like we going for picture" the AD said.

Paris and Kim stood together as he readied to handcuff her.

"Sound!" the director said.

"Rolling!" the sound assistant said.

"Camera rolling!" the assistant cameraman said.

A guy ran toward Vivaca and I with a clipboard he held it next to my hands as I cuffed Vivaca's wrist.

"Bounty Hunter take one scene one Paris hands cuffs to Kim" the assistant director said.

"And . . . action!" the director said.

I jerked Vivaca around opened the handcuffs then pushed her down on the bed when that happened she stopped the scene.

"OH HELL NO! This is not working for me! This feels like were making a porno, the handcuffs then pushing my ass down on the bed no, no, no, this doesn't work for me Tony!" Vivaca said.

"Alright people back to one" the first AD said.

"Hunters revenge, take two . . . scene one . . . Paris hookin' up with Kim" the assistant director said.

". . . . and action!" Tony said.

Paris was standing behind Kim taking the cuffs off; he pulled her towards him kissed her on the neck. She turned around looked at him and stretched her neck sideways reaching with her lips to kiss Paris in a playful like manner. Vivaca led Paris to the bed, as she stood in front of him. Slowly Paris began to ascend down on to the bed while Vivaca changes her position where she climbs on top of him. She began kissing his chest and worked her way up to his lips, where she planted a passionate sensuous wet kiss on his lips that lasted for about a good long sixty seconds.

"And . . . cut! Check the gate" Tony said.

When the scene was over everyone applauded the passionate scene it was hot.

"Checking the gate" the assistant director said.

Tony and I looked at the monitor of what was just shot Tony liked what he saw and wanted to set up for the next shot.

"Okay, I like it when we're rolling like this if we keep this up we'll be out of here early. We're moving on" Tony said.

"Okay people were moving on. Let's get the next set up bring Paris and Kim's stand-in's to the set now were sending Jonathan and Vivaca to their trailers. We'll send for them when we're done setting up for the next scene . . ." the first AD said.

I walked over to where Vivaca was sitting and congratulated her for the great work she had done. The AD brought my puppy.

"Just wanted to acknowledge your great work I think I can learn a lot from you" I said.

"You're not bad yourself; I think can learn a few things from you! Was that a set of keys in your pocket or were you just glad to be working with me? "Vivaca asked.

I was a little embarrassed about what had happened Mr. Willie never wakes up like that I thought I had better control than that I guess not.

"My bad just a little nervous that has never happen to me before" I said.

"There's always a first time for everything, Jonathan" Vivaca said.

"You right I just needed to relax and take my time" I said.

"You'll get the hang of it soon . . . The more you and I work together soon everything will just fall right into place you know what I mean? Together you and I Will work it out" Vivaca said.

"Hey Jonathan I got to make a run here's your puppy, I'll get her from you when I get back unless you want to let her go with me?" the AD said.

"That's okay I'll keep her you go handle your business I want to play with her thanks for keeping her" I said.

The AD left Vivaca looked at the puppy and fell in love with her.

"Ah he so cute! Can I hold him?" Vivaca said.

I handed the puppy to Vivaca she laughed as DOG licked her face.

"Oh, he is just so adorable! I think he likes me!" Vivaca said.

"It's a girl, you know children and animals know when people have good spirits" I said.

Vivaca picks up the puppy to see if it was a boy or a girl "Yeah It's a girl alright, well I'm glad we are done shooting that scene for today because I think she just peed on my dress . . . ?" Vivaca said.

# ANOTHER SAD DAY

Cars entered into the Rose Hills Cemetery and parked near the front entrance. In the center of the graveyard was a pond with ducks and white swans. People stood near a gravesite around the casket there were six chairs lined up in front of the pastor as he delivered his words of comfort. Over a hundred people came to say their last goodbye's to Shane Hilton. Bernard, Gerald, Sandy and I stood with the family as the pastor ended the service.

The participants bowed their heads as the pastor prayed over the grave. "Another sad day it's time for Shane to go home he is survived by his wife Janice Hilton; a six-year-old daughter Tina Hilton and Jonathan Paul his cousin. We were all created from the earth and when our work is done The Father calls us home. Dust to dust and ashes to ashes. Bow your heads please. Almighty Father one of your sons has gone home to be with you we ask that you to continue to watch over his wife daughter and family members. Protect them as they continue to move forward with their lives you have provided for us the one and only solution for our sin. We want to thank you for sending your son Jesus Christ to the cross to cleanse us with His Blood we know Shane is in a better place. All who agree say . . ."

"Amen . . . Amen and Amen." The people responded I walk over to the casket and put a white rose on top of it family members cried out. Shane's death represented a part of me that no longer existed this is my way of making a change in my life; Shane's death was closure for me. That mean and evil person was gone forever and laid to rest. Sandy stood by my side Bernard and Gerald stood nearby and waited for Sandy and I to finish saying our last good byes. After the service concluded, people stayed and talked to one another then slowly they all dispersed as they entered their cars and drove off. The funeral escorts stopped traffic allowing cars to leave the cemetery in single file down the road.

Just west of Rose Hills was a restaurant called Coco B Palms It was the place where the extras and small groups of people hung out and waited to get paid. It was just another sad day when it's all said and done you keep it pushin' to the next level it's funny how karma has a way of stepping into our lives and shows us what's really going on.

Later that night, DL's father took a late night swim in his large swimming pool. After swimming three laps he got out of the water one of his servants stood nearby with a beach towel in his hand. Larry grabbed the towel dried his head and then took a seat next to where his personal bartender was set up. Larry took a deep breath as he settled into his chair it kind of looked like he was out of breath a little.

"Would you like something to drink?" the bartender asked.

"Yea, why not I'm sure not getting back in that water anytime soon tonight. That was it for me . . . I'm getting old man! Know what I really want to do? Don't laugh, I want to go fishing go to a concert in the park you know settle down with some beautiful young lady and enjoy life" Larry said.

"You can do that Larry you can do whatever you want. You can write your own paycheck for the rest of your life, man I think settling down would do you well. Maybe it's time to pass the crown over and let the new blood run the organization" the bartender said.

"You know, that's real talk! First I need to find someone in the family to complete what Joey was suppose to do. Since he was a little boy I knew he was not cut out for this business yeah, he tried real hard to prove to me that he was inflexible. I thought he would work out only because he had my blood running through his veins. It never dawned on me that he took his mother's side of the bloodline weak. Well, I brought him into this world, and I took him out it was for his own good" Larry said.

"Larry, did I hear right? You killed Joey? Your own son?" the bartender said.

"Look, don't get it twisted I love all my children but you must understand something I'm a businessman first. I created this family so that if something were to happen to me some other capable family member could take over and run things. And yes, I did kill my own son, you want to know why? Joey had been a failure all of his life, time and time again I was always getting him out of sticky situations with the family that made people in high places question my ability to be in charge of running this operation. He was given a job to do and he didn't carry out. Now if other family members see me letting him get away with shit just because he was my son, I can't go out like that I have a rep to protect it's about the

Brotherhood one for all and all for one. Other member's would began to think they could do the same thing. Everyone in this family is treated equally if I hadn't done anything about it, people would begin to talk and we don't need that do we? I'M THE SHOT CALLER! And it's going to stay that way until I LEAVE HERE IN A PINE BOX!" Larry said.

"You gotta do what you have to do to keep order. Hey I understand totally my man, some people think it's a game we play out here, but let it be known, we all make choices in life. Some are good and some are bad," the bartender said.

"Well, Joey made a bad one AND HE PAID FOR IT WITH HIS LIFE!" Larry said.

Larry took the fresh drink that the bartender made and took a sip he sat back in his seat then took another sip when he was hit with sharp shooting pains up and down his left arm. As he held the drink in his left hand, suddenly he dropped it. As the drink fell to the ground Larry grabbed and held his chest with his eyes bucked as he gasped for air. The bartender called 911.

"911 what is your emergency?" the dispatcher said.

"My friend is having a heart attack" the bartender said.

"I'm sending help sir don't move him just make sure to try and keep him comfortable" the dispatcher instructed.

"Okay he seems to be able to breathe a little better now but appears to be in a lot of pain" the bartender Said.

"The Paramedics are arriving at your address, where are you and the patient located now?" the dispatcher asked.

"We're in the backyard by the pool area" he replied.

The paramedics rushed into the back yard. One of them talked to Larry as another checked his vital signs another paramedic brought a stretcher while two paramedics lifted Larry up and placed him on the stretcher. They put him in the ambulance and rushed him off to the hospital. The bartender called Butch, Tony and Samaria to let them know their father had just experienced a heart attack, and that he was being transported to St. Gabriel Hospital.

Four hours later Larry was in the intensive care unit. The right side of his heart had collapsed so they had to open Larry up go inside and correct the problem the surgery was successful. Larry laid motionless in the hospital bed. Butch, Tony and Samaria all stood around their father's bed. They all waited for him to open his eyes. Butch couldn't take seeing his father in that condition so he sat near the foot of his father's bed praying that his health becomes better.

Four men wearing black suits walked in the room three of them stood by the door. The alpha dog of the pact walked over to Larry's bed and looked down on him with a smirk on his face. He was a five foot nine inch hot headed jarhead and he was Larry's right hand man now that the old man was resting he thought he could start running things his way. Butch didn't like Curtis because Curtis was always trying to call shots without his father's permission Butch wanted him to understand that the only person that would run things after his father's death was someone of the Bush Love bloodline.

"I told him two months ago to see a doctor he was complaining about chest pains then. You rest now I'll make sure things run smoothly while you're resting" Curtis said to Larry.

"You know what? You're not running a damn thing you always run around trying making people think your next in line to run this family. This is my family's business! This goes deeper than you think Potner. Allow me to let you in on a secret if anything happens to my father someone of HIS bloodline will be in charge you feel me. I wouldn't get my hopes up too high so just kick back, and do what you do flunkie!" Butch said.

Curtis knew Butch was right he always laid in the cut waiting for the moment to make his move. Larry suddenly woke up just before Butch was about to punch Curtis in the face.

"What is going on? I could hear everything the two of you were talking about! First of all I'm not going anywhere secondly I will choose the next shot caller I'm in charge of this family! Do I make myself clear?" Larry said.

Samaria got up walked over to Butch and Curtis and pushed them out of the room.

"What the Hell's wrong with the two of you? Are you trying to kill the man? He just had a triple bypass heart surgery and the two of you are arguing like two old bitches! Curtis you and Butch need to chill out and stop trippin what the two of you are doing does not prove a DAMN THING. Now the two of you go on back in there and act like you got some sense" Samaria said.

Curtis entered the room and Butch and Samaria followed.

"I don't like that brotha'! He really thinks dad is going to let him take over and run the family business! That not's happen over my dead body" Butch said.

"I know how you feel, but this is not the time or place for that conversation" Samaria said.

Everyone calmed down and Larry motioned for Curtis to come to him. Curtis leaned over to hear what Larry had to say. Curtis walks over to the door where the mob brothers were standing. One of them gave Curtis three manila envelopes from his briefcase Curtis looked at Butch and handed the envelopes to Larry who then handed each of his kids an envelope. They looked at one another and removed the contents. Butch Tony and Samaria had just received their first job. They looked at their picture then looked at their Father it was a picture of their brother DL.

Samaria just received a call on her cell phone it was her brother DL, from time to time he and his baby sister would chop it up on the phone. DL stood on a balcony with a green apple martini in hand and Standing right beside him was Robin the American Airlines flight attendant; all snuggled up with him somewhere in the south of France.

"Hey baby girl! What's crackin?" I've been a little under the weather trying to keep it all together but you know you can't keep a good brother down very long . . . How you been baby girl'?" DL said.

"Not so well, just another sad day. DL . . . Pop just had a heart attack it's not looking good for the old man" Samari said.

"He just WHAT? WHAT HOSPITAL IS HE IN SAM?" DL said in a panic.

At St. Gabriel's hospital here in LA. POP's in critical conditions DL . . . where are you? Samaria said.

# ABOUT THE AUTHOR

Paul L. Higgins was born in Kansas City Missouri. He grew up in Compton California. At first writing was a hobby in Jr. High. Then in High School writing became a part of him. Paul Played in the marching band as second trumpet, and was active in drama class as a Thespian. He graduated from Domiguez High school in 1974. In 1976 Paul studied cosmetology and would later become responsible for the look of the group "Switch" and Jermaine Jackson's, "Let's get Serious" album cover. Later in 1980 Paul would go on the "Tiger Flower Tour" with "Switch" as they became a house whole name. Paul worked for Motown from 1979-1983. As a actor, speaker, writer, storyteller and a composer of music Paul's talents has given him extensive experience in the movie industry. Paul has been a member of the Screen Actors Guild and ASCAP since 1994. Paul is also active in the Ministry at St. Paul Evangelical Lutheran Church in Los Angeles where he serves as a minister of music. In 2007 Paul recorded his first single "Love Me". And in his spare time he is active in coaching baseball with at-risk youth for his community.

Community service is very important to Paul. He supports organizations such as the YMCA and the Department of Social Services, along with the Foster Parenting Association.

Paul Was a student at American film Institute in 2002, where he studied to be a director of films. In 2007, Paul has uploaded on the Internet the first all Afro-American soap Opera on Youtube Titled "Paternal Longings" and a Video poetry entitled "The Face of Crazy". Networking, Politics and charity drives surround his everyday activities. Paul is currently a bachelor and resides in Los Angeles.